Praise for Josh Patrick Sheridan

"*The Four Deaths of Clayton Standard* is a gorgeous, brutal story. Sheridan's voice is gritty, mordant, invested in the rich texture of Appalachian culture. His characters embody the true complexities of life in the region. The dialogue, alone, was enough to make me homesick."

—Todd D. Snyder, author of *The Rhetoric of Appalachian Identity*

"Sheridan's *The Four Deaths of Clayton Standard* is at turns a poignant, haunting, timely, bleak, and profound exploration of masculinity—as well as the ways a commitment to masculinity can go horribly wrong. Set in turn-of-the-last century Appalachia, and evoking such classics as *Brokeback Mountain* and *Ethan Frome*, this story of love and lives lost to love is a lyrical gem of a book that will stick with you for a long, long time."

—Rone Shavers, author of *Silverfish*

The Four Deaths of Clayton Standard

Josh Patrick Sheridan

APRIL GLOAMING

Publisher's Cataloguing-in-Publication Data

Sheridan, Josh Patrick
    The four deaths of clayton standard / written by Josh Patrick Sheridan
    ISBN: 978-1-953932-15-0

1. Fiction: General 2. Fiction: Southern - General I. Title II. Author

Library of Congress Control Number: 2022951356

For Penelope

THE TIMBER CAMP FOREMAN, whose name was Clifford Haymarket but whose men called him Chief, had just hiked his britches after a sharp and watery crap when he heard a commotion come over the hill. Worried that his dogs had gotten into the bramble again and run across a porcupine, or maybe a fisher cat, he snapped on his suspenders and stuffed his toes into the wet nethers of his boots and hiked the crest trail downward toward the bank of Cranberry Creek, the scrappy end of a handrolled cigarette sizzling between his lips and his Remington 1900 cracked open against his shoulder.

The forest bottom here was dark and foreign, though it was nearly a decade since the company had stumbled across a quarter million acres of virgin timber untouched and unspoken-for. Here, in this way-back place, stood granddaddy poplars, hickories, sycamores, cities of red spruce with their arms spread over the sky. As Chief made his descent to the water, he almost wished he'd brought along his lantern, though it was not yet noon—such was the depth of the blackness, the efficiency of the trees in keeping sun from striking earth. A man could stretch his hammock here and look to the sky and believe the tiny pockmarks of light that slipped through the canopy were constellations of stars, that his day had somehow gotten away from him and become evening, or worse: that his entire world had fallen into eternal nighttime. But then a tree would be felled, and the man's toes and britches would be washed over in a haze of blazing sunlight, and a great shining burst of dust and insect wings and sweat from the brows of men standing close would swell into the newfound void and spin upward like a funnel cloud. All involved would, for a minute or two, remember that they were living on Earth and not, as they might have begun to suspect, on the surface of the moon.

The hoots and yowls that drew Chief through the darkness were not those of dogs and their cornered prey but of men: a circle of lumberjacks standing bare-chested in a spotlight of sun that fell on Cranberry Creek, watching a pair of their company jockey with each other, ankle-deep in water, for the upper hand in a fistfight.

Goddammit, Standard, Chief thought, sneaking toward the rowdy sideshow with his head cocked owl-like and his fingers swelling around the Remington's action. His boy, Clayton Standard, a stray and a piss-bucket who drew more deeply than others from the limited well of Chief's fondness, was a notorious scrapper; the kid could conjure a beef from anything and could never settle it without the swift and savage use of his fists and knees and, occasionally, the weathered kettle that was his forehead. An ugly son of a bitch that Chief had first laid eyes on the night the boy tried to sleep off a drunk inside another man's tent, having slithered into camp like a snake on his way to hell or some other near-enough place, Standard had been born with a cleft lip that some backwater surgeon had fashioned into a kind of permanent sneer, a thick-scalped, mulish head, and a pair of gray eyes that recalled cindered coal. (Because the kid clearly had guts, and because he was short on men anyway, Chief had felt more or less obligated to hire him on, and since then Standard had swung a strong ax and took kindly enough to KP and saved many a man's life with his great booming voice calling *"TAMberrrrrr!"* whereupon a tremendous forest giant, standing sometimes two hundred years, would come crashing to its knees and scare an honest worker's guts up into his mouth.)

The problem with Standard wasn't the work ethic but the temper.

The sounds of the tussle in the creek came back to Chief in fits: the piggish grunting; the slapping of footbottoms in the water like children in the bath; the whooping of the circled timbermen, placing bets, calling out sympathies when slugs landed flush. The entire forest echoed with the effort. Chief selected a large hemlock to crouch behind and quietly slid a cartridge into his gun. It was his practice to allow the boys to sort themselves out with minimal interference from management, knowing that a natural pecking order—and a healthy sense of one's place in it—was ever-helpful to the efficiency-minded gaffer.

Besides, for a campfire disagreement to come to fisticuffs was common enough; these were stout men of resolute constitution, after all. Men raised in a world where one defended himself regardless of circumstance. Hard-knock boys whose childhood teachers had been hunger, violence, and disappointment. The majority of Chief's company made of younger men, men in their twenties and early thirties, who still believed—despite a bulging and relentless lack of evidence—that life would soon enough get better, that their fortunes were bound to change, that a Model-T and a two-bedroom house and the sweet, wide-hipped keeper of the family recipe box were only matters of time. For the veterans in camp, these men had lost their minds: the older fellows knew there was no goodness in life but the sound of a treetrunk snapping in twain, the pouty-mouthed lapping of a snared brook trout, a cigarette by the campfire and a good-natured story of the rustic whore someone came across in Gatlinburg who could whistle with her armpits and would fix her customers a batch of red-eye gravy if they paid to stay until morning. These two brands of men—the hopeful and the hopeless—came to blows often, because their opposing viewpoints sucked all the air from the sky and left their compatriots no recourse but to fight back in order to keep from suffocating.

The lumberjacks shifted their big bodies around Clayton Standard and the fellow he was scuffling with, a slender Pennsylvania Dutch boy named Glick. The fight churned this way and that. Chief watched through the zoetrope spaces between their shoulders and legs and saw Standard land a jab on Glick's jaw that sent the boy reeling for purchase across the creekbed. The men erupted, and their cheer spread through the undergrowth and ricocheted from tree trunks like a firework.

It turned out the boy Glick had a funny habit: he would square himself up and face Standard and then lift his leading leg slightly out of the water as though he were afraid of stepping on a snake. He'd hold his fists in front of himself as a boxer would but keep that leg dangling in front like a swollen pecker, his back foot jammed down into the cobbles for balance.

Why on earth, Chief thought. How had a boy like Glick run afoul of an ogre like Standard? Had the kid no sense? Standard's advantage was one of at least eighty pounds, six inches, and miles of stupidity. He'd won a hundred fights more vicious than anything Glick had even heard about. Nervous, Chief shifted from one knee to the other, leaning his weight into the stock of his Remington, and watched through the crowd as Standard dropped his guard and began to laugh heartily, making a show of his good nature, pointing at the Glick boy's posture. It seemed for a second that the fight might even have ended; Standard's hands were loose beside his hips and his head was tilted back to the sky. His thick throat stretched with laughter. His Adam's apple bobbed up and down. His mouth fell open so wide Chief could see the gaps where clusters of rotten teeth had been removed, and his laughter was a haunting noise: a garbled *huh-huh-huh* charging through layers of snot and a persistent film of tobacco smoke. It was a laugh filtered through all of the great man's horrific childhood memories and belched into the air, sounding at once like happiness and unbearable grief. To Chief, it recalled the lamented sobbing of an idiot whose puppy has just been trampled by a horse.

But then, in the middle of this outburst of jollity, the wounded Glick boy, ignored momentarily to become the butt of their humor, leapt straight up from the creekbed like a crane taking wing, the water geysering around his hips, and brought his rear leg up and swung it in a tight arc that clipped the hatbrims of the men around him. His foot caught Clayton Standard directly in the windpipe, and the pathetic laughter stopped with a splintered, hacking cough. Standard stood wide-eyed, clutching his neck and sucking desperately for air, before he fell to his knees and finally collapsed face-first into the water. As the stupefied timbermen watched, unable to say anything coherent, Glick leapt onto Standard's back and shoved the giant's big stupid mouth farther down into the rubble of the creekbed, really mashing it in, rocking the head back and forth as though he were dredging a hole in the silt.

Chief finally shouldered the Remington and aimed at the sky and ripped off a shot. The startled men broke apart and turned to stare at him, and Chief got his first good view of the Glick boy—scrawny and frightened and, judging by his puny blonde beard, no more than seventeen or eighteen—and there at his feet lay the body of Clayton Standard, cutting a rift in the current like a stone rolled down from the mountainside and come to its violent rest in the sweet cool water of Cranberry Creek.

THE NIGHT STANDARD FIRST SLUNK INTO CAMP, there was a blue gibbous moon. It was a Saturday, and most of the men had taken the train into Summersville to spend their newfound wealth on booze and country women. They'd return the next day in time for ten-thirty lunch, and though the invitation to join was always open, Chief chose not to fraternize with his men in that way. He was no good at holding his liquor, and anyway, the dogs needed fed and the equipment needed watching over. What he didn't tell anyone, not a single soul, was that he spent his beloved Saturday evenings reading in his hooch: Melville, Hemingway, Fitzgerald, books he kept inside his pillowcase and packed away in his foot locker as soon as they were finished.

It was *This Side of Paradise* that lured him into that particular cool evening, where he popped his canvas chair and lit his lamp and sat groaning in that strange, pleasurable way one does after a hard day's labor. The dogs lay in the dirt, jangling their floppy ears in protest of the bugs. When they finally slept, they whimpered and flinched, hastening after an imaginary quarry. *Fat old beasts,* Chief thought, though he loved his dogs dearly. He respected them for their courage and appreciated their honesty.

Experience, he read in Fitzgerald, *is the name so many people give to their mistakes.*

At first, the sleeping dogs didn't notice the bulbous shadow lumbering down the road, its thick feet clopping on the clay, metal bangles tinkling on its belt. It was a hundred yards away or more and hard to make out. Chief scrambled to hide the book under his lap-blanket, but the closer the shadow came, the surer he was that it was not one of his men; it was, in fact, nobody he recognized. This creature wore his hair long and uncombed, had broad shoulders and a thick neck, and every few seconds would whistle a descending tune—a series of three sharp, high-pitched tones, quite akin to the lonely call of a bird. Over the course of the few minutes Chief watched him coming on, the man must have whistled the cadence thirty times, as though it were the only piece of music he'd ever memorized. When the dogs finally startled, Chief hushed them with a snap of his fingers. The man stopped on the road and peered through the darkness to where Chief was sitting, to where the dogs lay with their hackles up, growling at him and clenching their claws against the dirt. They might have locked eyes, Chief and this strange newcomer, were it not for so much darkness between them.

The shadow turned from the road then and stumbled over a small culvert and into the camp proper, disappearing and reappearing as he moved among the tents. Chief watched him open the flap of each one, the rustle of canvas as he rummaged inside, the grunt of disapproval when he came away empty-handed. Finally, he went into Gary Childress's hooch, rustled around for a minute, and never re-emerged.

If there was a reason Chief hadn't stopped him, hadn't immediately set the dogs running and come in headlong with a double-load of buckshot ready, he didn't know what it was. Fear, perhaps, of a man who could be so bold as to enter an operation such as theirs and assume a natural place there, of a man who would whistle such a simple and haunting tune over and again, of a man who would be walking down such a road at such a time in the first place—it was half past eleven, after all, and they were fifteen miles from anywhere. Yes, it could have been fear. It could also have been curiosity; fear and curiosity (say the snake-handlers, and the cliff-divers, and the godforsaken newlyweds) being closely related. Chief might simply have wanted to understand the constitution of a man that would create such a challenge for himself, and therefore, had been reluctant to run him off. One cannot witness the breadth of the bear's paws if one first scares her away with his shouting.

He ran a line through the dogs' collars and tied them to a stump and picked up his Remington and walked slowly out into the field of tents pitched across the tilting, rooted ground. He hoped for a snore to burst free from one of them, or the sound of men slapping cards onto an overturned crate, but it seemed that every man in camp had retired that night to Summersville—even the old surly hands who thought little of a young man's brand of fun. There would be no aid tonight in dealing with this drunken intruder. Chief came down carefully, glancing back now and then to see that his lamp was still burning on its post, that the dogs were still secured. Then, momentarily losing care for where his feet were, he tripped on a tent stake and nearly tumbled head-over, but he caught himself with a great effort and let forth an accidental curse: "Goddammit!"

"That's takin the Lord's name in vain," a voice said.

Chief stopped short. "Who's that?" he said. He swung the Remington to his shoulder and aimed it into the nighttime.

"Who's the *Lord?*" the voice said. It was coming from Childress's tent: the shadow.

Chief pressed the barrel of the shotgun against the canvas. "Whyn't you come on outta there," he said, hopeful he was keeping his voice steady.

From inside, the shadow used his fingertips to push the gun gently away. The effect was that of a mouse trapped under a newspaper. "Come, now, that ain't necessary, is it?"

"Your life don't mean nothing to me, mister," Chief said, and pulled the hammers. "And neither does this tent." He leaned his weight onto his back leg and tightened the muscles in his chest.

But then the tent jostled abruptly upward as though a grenade had exploded inside and its front flap shot open and the shadow flashed free from his confines bare-assed and with a loose pile of clothes stuffed into the crook of his arm. His big body navigated the wide forest like a native beast, leaping gracefully over thick knuckles of root, bouncing from tree trunks and using the carom to change direction, his shoulders hunched against a shot he must have thought was coming, but which never did.

In fact, Chief had lowered the gun by then and held it by his hip, a useless, hollow twig. Watching the man run gave him the impression that no aim could be true against such a creature. The shadow coursed like a naked grizzly born of the forest and living an entire life built around it. When his breathing settled and the thrum of his heart tempered itself in his ears, Chief could hear the galloping grunt the shadow emitted as he ran, long after he'd lost sight of him through the trees. He'd never gotten a good look at the face.

It was the work of six strong men to lift Standard's sopping body from the water. Chief stood watching, hopeful that what his churning insides knew for sure could not be read across his face and that the timbermen would not desecrate Standard's body in any irreversible way.

They struggled to heft the dead man onto the creekbank. His clothes hung loose as though from a backyard line and his long hair was wrapped around his cheeks and neck, mercifully concealing the swollen purple bruise from Glick's death-strike and giving Standard the appearance of a fish tangled in a net. They set him as gently as they could in a damp patch of marshgrass and stood around for a while smoking and deciding what to do with him. Various suggestions were made: that they bury him on the spot; that they build a pyre and burn him, so that his spirit could drift into the trees; that they search for his loved ones, whatever cave they might have lived in and whatever pale chameleons they may have been, so they might venture out to collect the body and dispose of it in whichever way their heathen religion required.

"He had no one else who loved him," Chief heard himself say, though he wished he hadn't.

There was also the issue of Glick, who'd been yoked up and dragged from the creek, looking as incredulous as everyone else. They made him hug a tree and bound his hands and hurled insults and flicked cigarette cherries at him. It was a half-hearted retribution: after all, they agreed they'd witnessed a fair fight, and they'd placed bets on the boy to lose it. (The one fool who'd bet otherwise, a fossil named Russo with bulldog jowls and long eyelashes and sun-browned skin like a tobacco leaf, leaned against a birch finishing his tally, double-checking his math and calling out payments to the new debtors trying to sneak past him without being seen.) Some of them had generated side wagers that Standard would break at least one of the boy's major bones—an arm or leg or rib— or else bite off an ear or a digit in the throes of battle. But now that Glick had bested their champion and seemed more or less none the worse for wear, they were unsure any punishment was necessary. One man sat on a mossy log and proclaimed loudly that to incarcerate the boy for what he'd done was to shoot a weasel for killing a snake.

Glick, too, was indignant. "What just occurred was a miracle!" he shouted, hugging the tree awkwardly, his cheek smushed into its bark and his backside thrust outward like a child about to be paddled. "I ain't never known how to do something like that in my life!"

"That's bullshit," one of the men called back. "A thing like that don't come from nowhere."

"I swear it!" Glick said. "It was like... divine inspiration!"

"Aw, horseshit," another man said.

And so forth.

The camp chaplain, whose name no one seemed to know but who answered kindly to Chappy, stepped forward. His long white hair was yellowed at the ends due to his perpetual habit of holding a cigarette against his chin like a critic considering a painting. He wore his mustache sheepdog-style over the lip and kept an earring in either lobe. When he wasn't ministering, he was an expert sawyer and had taught many a greenhorn how not to die in the woods. The men respected him.

"I may have known Clayton Standard better than any man here today," Chappy said.

Bullshit you did, thought Chief, kicking at the dirt.

"A very decent man," Chappy said. He pinched his cigarette between his fingers and brought his hands to his face, rubbed his mustache while smoke filtered beneath his glasses and up into the hair that hung low on his forehead. "He always carried a special sentiment for the water. In fact, he and I often stood in this very spot, discussing love, and life. What it meant to be happy. Whether or not there was really a God, and what it would mean to meet Him."

Chief rocked from one foot to the other. He knew full and well that Standard was neither decent nor happy, nor ever willing to entertain the notion of God.

"I suspect," Chappy went on, "that our friend Clayton is right now finding out for himself the sublime nature of God's House. In fact, I suspect the two of them are embracing just at this very moment." He stared theatrically at the sky for a second, dragged his cigarette, and returned to his notion: "I believe beyond any doubt that our friend is happy now."

Some of the men had removed their caps and held them over their hearts while Chappy spoke. The sun beat hard and their heads sopped with sweat. Despite what the old preacher said, none of them really knew anything; their lives were defined by long stretches of toil punctured by moments of arranged bliss paid for in advance. Their Heaven was a day's respite brought on by torrential rain, their God the suicide king waiting in a deck when their hand needed the run. They turned their minds to Calvary only when someone died, or, to a far lesser extent, when someone was born. Tomorrow they would selfishly miss the things Clayton Standard had brought to their lives—a bawdy joke now and then, a safe buck in a fistfight, a decent plate of biscuits and gravy—but they'd give no more consideration to where he was living now that he was dead than they had when he was alive, except to be quietly relieved that wherever it was, it wasn't with them.

Thanks to Chappy's creekside sermon, it was decided that they would bury Standard right there in the sandy earth. Someone had gone back up the hill and fetched a barrowful of shovels and mattocks and the men had begun digging and whistling and telling tentative and morbid jokes before anyone paid any further attention to the boy Glick, still cinched against the tree, his raw cheek bleeding down his neck and into the collar of his shirt. His chest pumped up and down with his sobbing. "Forgive me, Lord," he moaned. "Forgive me, Lord. Forgive me."

The men looked at Chief with pitiful faces and leaned into the handles of their tools.

"Turn him loose," Chief said, finally.

CHIEF SPENT THAT FIRST NIGHT restless in his tent, absent-mindedly scratching the dogs behind their ears, picking up his book and putting it back down, sipping at a glass of whiskey. He felt good that he'd managed to chase the strange beast away but was unsettled that it now knew where they were, and that their separate existences would by necessity become threats to each other. It wouldn't do to have such a fellow harassing their operation; the next time, Chief would have to be more decisive with his firepower.

Having slept no more than half an hour, he was grateful when the first light of dawn began to creep beneath his tent flap. The dogs wandered out into the dooryard—such as it was—and lifted their legs to the nearest tree stumps. Chief did the same, his hackles raised in the chilly morning air. A mist about that wasn't quite rain. He ducked into his hooch and came out with his buckle-backs and pulled them on.

It wasn't two minutes before he heard the whistling again. His heart nearly stopped. The dogs took off in a fit before he could grab them, and they ran between the tents with their tails stiff and high, barking and snarling and chopping at the air with their teeth. Chief followed as best he could. His legs were not as strong as they'd once been, so his run was a bumbling thing. He heard himself yelling a strange *"Hyah! Hyah!"* sound, both to slow the dogs and to try and scare away whatever they might find before he could get there to help them. He was halfway down the hill before he realized he'd forgotten his gun.

He didn't need it. The enormous man from last night had the dogs on their backs, and he was crouched in the mud beside them, laughing and running his thick hands over their bellies. They lolled their tongues from their mouths like drunks. The man was bare-chested, his dripping work shirt laid carefully along a branch. His hair was wet and combed. When he lifted his head to acknowledge Chief, the foreman was struck by how beautiful he was: his jaw set like a brick, the wolfish gray eyes, the tight scar at his lip that made his smile seem simultaneously deeper and more sarcastic.

"Got a little out of hand last night," he said, still scratching the dogs' chests. They wiggled and kicked like ticklish children.

"Y'all break away from there," Chief said.

"That ain't necessary, now," the man said. "They like me."

"Hyah!" Chief barked, and the dogs finally scuttled away.

The man sighed and stood then, and Chief nearly lost his breath. He was huge—far larger than he'd appeared the night before. Broad and graceful in his movements, his body bisected with muscle and the smooth ridges of burn wounds long since healed over. He crossed to where his shirt hung and took it down, wrung it tightly in his large hands and stretched it, still damp, over his body.

"I'm in need of work," he said. His voice was confident, though the cleft had left him with a noticeable lisp: *I'm thirching for thome work.* He stood with the straight-backed posture of a man who's learned respect through a life of hard lessons.

"Funny way of asking," Chief said. His hands clammy, and a throbbing in the back of his head.

"We all got our own stories," the man said.

He reminded Chief of a picture he'd once seen in a children's book: the story of a shipwreck, an uncharted island, a group of men devising ways to survive. Their leader was a sailor named Conifer—how he possibly remembered these things!—who was tall and handsome and whose body was like large river stones somehow cobbled together into the shape of a man. Conifer's illustrated smile was broad and toothy—insane, almost—

and his fists were raised, as though just off-page some foolish mutineer were preparing his challenge. The young Clifford Haymarket, bent and directionless child himself, had returned to that picture again and again, kept the book nearby though he'd long since forgotten the story. What he'd seen in the drawing was *perfection:* the statuary of an attentive God, a Creator who minded the details and wielded a precise hammer. Yes, this man on the creekbank reminded Chief very much of that jovial pirate, Conifer. The resultant feeling was both enthralling and unacceptable.

"I'll have to ask you to clear out," Chief said.

The man made a show of looking over Chief's shoulder, scanning the hillside, sniffing the air. "You're the foreman?" he said.

"I have a responsibility to keep a tight camp," Chief said. He couldn't believe how unconvinced he was by himself.

The man smiled. "Seems to me you have a responsibility to cut down as many trees as possible." He looked up to the sky. "Winter's not too far off. Things'll be slowing down. I'm sure you have your quota."

"I'm not hiring," Chief said.

"Find me an ax," the man said. "I believe I might change your mind."

THE SEASON TURNED SOON ENOUGH, and the men went on working despite the weather. Timber not something that could wait the winter out, so they chopped and chained and pulled and loaded, their fingers like hard nubs of ginseng root. Their breath called out in front of them when they talked and sang. Their facial hair crusted over with frost like frozen waterfalls, the meltwater dripping onto their plates at chowtime: it was a mark of pride to wear a beard so long it didn't completely thaw overnight. Their skin turned red and glowed brightly, especially their cheeks, which gave some of the younger boys the look of china dolls. These boys took the brunt of their bullying: *Sweetie, come here,* the older men would say, making smooching noises with their lips. *Sissy-pants, lover-girl.* They were not men of decency, not necessarily.

Chief felt the cold more harshly than he ever had before. It took him longer to roust himself from sleep, longer to cinch his boots, more patience to pull on his long-johns. His bones ached as though with fever, and he swore to Perkins, the camp medic, that he could actually *feel* the cold sludgy blood burbling in his veins. More than once he forgot to feed the dogs in the morning and, perhaps more concerning to his men, he developed his own habit of skipping meals. They noticed that he'd begun to lose weight and told him so with solemn faces; to work the wintertime forest undersized and underfed made a man too juicy a target for the Fates. (They especially feared curly-haired Atropos, whom someone had accidentally learned of in grammar school: at mealtime, each man made a small pinch of grub and set it on the side of his tray—a hopeful offering that she might, for just one more day, give him the gift of his life. If a man died, they joked that he must have tried to give her his creamed rice, because everyone knew Atropos despised creamed rice, and that no self-respecting lumberjack would insult her with it.)

Fates or no, Chief simply couldn't bring himself to eat. There were days when he felt so empty no plate of beans would ever fill him; other times he was full to bursting, his belly aching, his lungs swollen, his head pounding with every heartbeat. The pain on those days was excruciating, and though skipping work had never been his practice, he sometimes spent them in his hooch, covered over with blankets, and the men would move about their lives outside listening to him moan and carry on. Shaking their heads, feeling for him. They knew long before Chief did that he was not sick at all but caught in a desperate bout of mourning.

"That caterwaulin," someone at chow would say. "All night long. I'm the next hooch over. That caterwaulin, I mean, Jesus Christ."

Someone else: "Man's in pain. Sometimes ain't no cure for pain but callin it out."

"Sometimes ain't no cure for callin it out except a sock in the throat."

"Do what you gotta do."

"Do what you gotta do is right."

"I thought at one point it was them goddamn dogs howlin. Jesus Christ. Just awful, that caterwaulin."

They were airing private prescriptions of a man they'd long admired: it was clear that Chief and Standard had been in a kind of love that none of them had ever felt for themselves, but to acknowledge it out loud would have required them to lose their respect—such were the rules—and they weren't yet ready to do it.

The winter charged steadily toward spring. They saw Chief now and then, completing some duty of foremanship, jotting on his ledger, talking to the mechanic about a busted carburetor. He sat with them now and then in the mess, but he never ate; instead, he drank copious amounts of water, dipping into the pitcher again and again with his tin cup, slurping as though it contained the secrets of eternal life. When he came up for air, the whiskers of his mustache would be dripping, like a dog having lapped from a puddle. "Jesus, that's good," he would say. "That come from the creek, did it?"

It was during one of these meals that, after having gorged himself with water, Chief stood and reluctantly announced to the company that the coming spring would be his last. He had received word that his mother was ill and had decided to return to Greenbrier County after the thaw to see her well. So long as he accepted the post, Chief said, Gary Childress would become their new foreman. Chief's cheek trembled and he began to cry. "I don't know, and will never know, if this is the right thing to do," he said. "But I wish to say goodbye to each of you, individually," — and to a man they looked at his fingers, which had grown thin and frail and wrinkled, like those of an old witch, and wondered whether it would hurt him too badly if they shook his hand.

STANDARD WAS NO MORE OR LESS COMPETENT with an ax than the average greenhorn, but what he lacked in technique, he made up for in brutality: he swung great lops at the base of a hickory Chief pointed out, sending shards of wood the size of dictionaries from its loin and expelling a massive grunt with each blow.

"Stop, stop, stop," Chief said, after a few such licks. "Jesus Christ, you've got a cut, haven't you?"

"My daddy wasn't good for much," Standard said, "but he knew how to fell a tree."

Chief grunted. "Not if he done it like you're trying to do, he didn't." He reached for the ax and squared up and took a swing: the chip that flew away was sharp and triangular, a neat copy of the axhead. The divot it left in the hickory's meat seemed bound for some greater purpose. Where Standard was a child crushing ice with a pan, Chief was a sculptor carving eyelashes from stone. "You gotta treat her like a lady," he said. "You hit her firm and keep your aim true, she'll come when you want her to. You smash into her like a train, she's liable to turn around and spit in your face."

Standard smiled, his lip beautiful and horrible at once. He took the ax and tried again. His cut struck just a hair above the gap Chief's swing had left, shaving another wedge away.

"There it is," Chief said. "A tree this size'd take a hundred of my blows and six hundred of your'n. You want to show them muscles off six times to my one, you be my guest, but make sure ain't me or none of my men around when you do it. We'll just save you some chow for when you're done."

They took the hickory down together, trading blows from either side. Chief had pointed out where it would fall, and when it landed with a shudder in that exact spot, Standard looked at him and danced a tight little jig.

<hr>

IT STARTED TO RAIN ON THE FIFTEENTH OF MARCH. The men rested under the flaps of their hooches, smoking, calling out, eating beans straight from the can and drinking coffee from their tin cups. With so much rain, there wasn't much that could be done except to watch the snow melt under their feet and wonder how high the creek would get. They hung their shirts and undergarments on branches to wash off the grime and had competitions to see who could keep his bare toes in the meltwater longest without leaping out. The day passed into night and into the next day and in all that time, they hadn't gone to work on a single tree.

Chief whiled the break sitting on his locker with his legs crossed at the ankles, waiting for his man to come with a team and wagon to take him down off the mountain. He'd hired a fellow from Summersville and his two mules to lug the dogs and his small collection of clothing and knickknacks down into Greenbrier County, where Chief would meet his dying mother in the dooryard and come inside for a soup bowl of grits and wait for the old lady to die so that he could call himself a farmer and a landowner and forget the forest altogether.

In the evening of the deluge's second day, he wearied of waiting and stepped from his hooch and looked out over the camp: the tendrils of smoke from the small fires men kept burning under the canopies of finger-laced branches; in the distance, a fog so tight one could trace its path through the forest as it drifted along on the wind. The trees outstretched their arms and dripped water like women standing from a bath. (Chief had never had such a woman, and never would, but he'd heard many a tale of her—pornographic stories of her aromatic underparts, her curved spine, her various abilities in contorting herself to fit the needs of the moment. This woman came up often in camp, and Chief had always attempted to excuse himself when she did, but if that proved impractical, he made every effort to extract something of her beauty, rather than mere carnality, from the anecdote: while the men rocked back and forth on their perches, laughing through a description of the shape her mouth took in the throes of sexual fervor, Chief tried desperately to imagine what such a woman's favorite food might be, or what it may have sounded like when she told her daughter she loved her.)

The crack of men shouting broke through the rain.

"Pierce, for fuck's sake!" someone said from inside his hooch.

"What's that?"—someone else, probably Pierce.

"Kill the canary, would you? Today ain't the day."

"What's that? Whose canary?"

A third: "Boys, a little peace, please. Jesus Christ, I'm trying to sleep."

And a fourth: "Trying to stretch the bishop, more likely."

"So what if I am?"

"Hey, we're all at the same business."

Pierce again: "I wasn't doing nothing. Fuck the lot of you."

The first man: "You were whistling."

"Like hell I was."

And then, just as suddenly, the disagreement died down again, and there was nothing but the sound of the forest: the patting of raindrops on deadfall, a man's grunting footsteps on his way to the latrine, the intermittent cracking sound of waterlogged limbs finally giving way. Chief could hear the gurgle of Cranberry Creek, six or seven feet higher the last time he checked, and he quietly mused that the line of weathered men who stood fishing on its newfound banks were likely having decent luck on a day like today.

But again, the shouting broke loose:

"Pierce, now goddammit, if you don't finish whistling that tune, I'm gonna finish it for you!"

He recognized the voice this time as that of Gary Childress, his second-in-command. A unique talent with a blade and a terribly hard-driven man, Childress once told Chief the origin story of his work ethic: his father had been a hatter before the turn of the century, and at one point held a contract with the United States Navy to fashion campaign hats for men on their way to Cuba and the Philippines. A twelve-year-old Childress was recruited to help in the overwhelmed tannery, and over the next six months, he suffered terrible burns to his face and forearms. To this day, his hands, when he unfurled them, were stained red like rusty metal, and the pinkies, though usable, could not extend more than partway. Those six months in the tannery informed Childress's entire theory of business: a man needed his wood for burning the same as he needed his hat for the war, and where there was need there was work, and where there was work there would be money, and where there was money there would be Gary Childress. Which is to say, he didn't much care for the time-thirsty entertainments men in camp were prone to devising, and he certainly did not suffer whistling.

Chief saw the flap of Pierce's tent whip open and watched the sleep-drunk boy stumble into the evening. "Call me a liar again, I'll fucking kill you," Pierce said to no one. His hair was far-flung and filthy, and his voice sounded like smoke.

Then there was Perkins, and Chappy, and several other men working their way to the clear spot where Pierce had chosen to stand his ground. They were happy for the prospect of a fight, especially if that fight was to feature Childress, Chief's apparent successor. There had been a sort of moratorium on violence since that August day when Glick killed Clayton Standard, and the feeling seemed to be that it was high time to start it up again. If the question to be settled was as simple as a man's proclivity for songbirding, so be it. The cause was far less important than the solution.

Chief watched the men filter in—it suddenly seemed everyone in camp would bear witness—and collapse around Pierce and Childress, the air full of that ursine hormone men excrete when they've excited themselves over violence. He picked up his Remington, just as he'd done on the day Standard died, and made his way carefully toward the ring, readying himself to play referee if things got out of hand. He stood in the back beside a pair of fishermen come up from the water, their catches still dangling life-like from strings tied at the belt.

The group hushed. Indiscreet handfuls of bills circulated this way and that. Whispers that landed on shoulders, quick handshakes. They breathed as a collective, their boots digging a circle in the mud as they jockeyed for purchase on the hillside, grabbing at sapling branches and each other's clothing. Their eyes darting like madmen, scanning the combatants, scouring their faces for signs of weakness and confidence. Chief watched the ugly scene and kept his wad in his pocket. It seemed the good money was on Childress, but if he'd learned anything, it was not to bet against the rube.

No blows fell. Instead, inside of that quiet moment when Pierce and Childress went about sizing each other up, while each of them jutted his lip and clenched and unclenched his fists, a song pierced the air: a whistled song of three notes, blown in descending order over and over again, a tune with no apparent end that came, improbably, from everywhere.

THEY SPENT THE REST OF THE MORNING making biscuits for the men, who would return soon on the train from Summersville. They would stumble over the horizon like a herd of cattle, milky-eyed and braying, singing the names of passionate women, crowing over poker winnings, punching each other in the shoulders. Their hangovers would be raging, but overall, their respite will have been good for them, and with the addition of a good plate of country gravy, Chief could be sure to get a worthwhile afternoon's work in.

"You wanna pull some water for coffee, or yank them biscuits out of the fire?" he asked Standard, who was tending the bake-oven like a child waiting to open a Christmas present.

"I'll stay here and mind the oven," Standard said. He had a strange penchant for excitement, this big man: the fallen tree had given him no small amount of joy, and the rising biscuit dough had spread an infantile grin across his face. At first, Chief had not gotten the impression that Standard was especially limited, mentally speaking, but more and more he had to wonder. Chief had spent his entire adult life around men who relished simple pleasures, but Standard's enthusiasm seemed different. It was as though he did not simply enjoy childish things but was, in reality, a child himself.

The men roared into the mess with the clamor of a circus breaking camp. Their songs and shouts and snorts, their derision and self-deprecation, their commitment to a netherworld full of lady parts and psychotropics: a full display of pleasures, primitive and indisputable. Most of them probably had not slept a single hour the night before, except possibly with their drunken heads leaned against the man beside them on the train; still, their energy was palpable and intimidating. They made a raucous noise even without meaning to. Standard poked his head out of the kitchen doorway and smiled.

"They'll enjoy this," he said.

Chief's younger brother growing up had been dim-witted. Gerald Haymarket, born nearly three months premature and runtish in stature, slowed by bowlegs like the gnarled limbs of apple trees. He was a miraculous gift to their mother, who hated Clifford's sense of independence and the smart lip that came along with it, who could at least take Gerald's hand and manipulate it around the handle of a pitcher, who could guide his fingers through the dusty coat of a lamb, who put the back of his wrist to her forehead when she was sweating, so he knew she was alive and well and working to keep him fed. Gerald and his mother were as inseparable as twins: she took him along to the creek to do the washing, sat with him in his weekly bath in the backyard tub, read a book in the rear of the schoolhouse during the first and only day of his formal education. ("I can't service your boy," their teacher, Mr. Holyoke, had confessed at dismissal, while young Clifford sat on the other side of the room looking at his brother's dumb face and burning fiercely in his desire to choke Mr. Holyoke to death.) Their mother saw in Gerald a plaything and a blank slate: he bore none of the casual mistrust that mars common relationships, and so their relationship was not common. Thus, Clifford sat on the sidelines for most of his childhood while his mother forgot about him in favor of his younger brother. Now, watching Clayton Standard's excitement over a pan of lumpy dough, he realized for the first time that his mother was never really to blame for anything.

When he emerged from the kitchen with a pitcher of coffee for each table, Chief's men greeted him heartily:

"Cheers for watching 'er over," they said,

"One of these days, we'll convince you to come along,"

"You don't know what you're missing,"

"And even if you do, there's no sense in missing it again."

He walked among them, patting them on their broad shoulders, smiling and demurring, loosely readying them for another week of work. The men were disgusting on Sundays, great heaving barrels of bovine sacrilege. They smelled of barnyard sex. Their shirts were stained through with sweat, their hair damp and musty and cocked at odd angles. It was all Chief could do to keep his breath. When he came to a man named Gilroy, he patted his shoulder and Gilroy looked up at him.

"Whassa madder, Chief?" Gilroy said, still drunk. The gin burned in his throat and shone on his teeth.

"It's good to see you in one piece, Gilroy," Chief said.

"One piece!" Gilroy shouted, and snorted a laugh. "Not so long ago, you'da seen me in one piece, and then another, and then another still!"

Chief looked at him blankly for a second and made to move on, but Gilroy snatched him by the wrist.

"Whassa madder, Chief?" he said again. "You don't get it? *Piece?*"

"I get it," Chief said. "Get an extra biscuit in that gullet, why don't you."

Gilroy's grip tightened. "You don't get it," he said. He looked at the men at his table. "He doesn't get it."

"Turn him loose," someone said.

"He's a pansy," Gilroy said.

"Gilroy, I said turn him loose."

But Gilroy only twisted his fingers tighter around Chief's arm. "I'm hurt that you don't like my joke," he said.

There was a crashing sound from the direction of the kitchen, and the men turned to see Clayton Standard, huge and heaving, an upturned rack of biscuits at his feet. He took thick, clomping steps toward Gilroy, who quickly released his hold on Chief's wrist and stood to defend himself.

"Who the fuck is this?" Gilroy said. He couldn't take his eyes off the beast bearing down on him. He raised his fists half-heartedly and the spectating men, who were also seeing Clayton Standard for the first time and had no better idea what was happening than Gilroy did, quickly jabbered their advice:

"Two steps back, Gilroy!"

"Get them fists tight, he's coming!"

"Tuck your chin!"

"Take what he gives you!"

They watched, half-standing, half-sitting, as Standard stepped within arms' reach of Gilroy. Up close, his true advantage came clear: a man of Gilroy's size could have slid his entire body into the sleeve of Clayton Standard's jacket. Standard bested him by a foot or more. His pulpy fists were each nearly as big as Gilroy's head, and the cheaply-fashioned shoes on his feet were about the length of Gilroy's arm from fingertip to elbow.

Standard snatched Gilroy by the shirt collar and shook him like a snared fish. He raised his other hand above the poor fool's head, and there was a terrible pause that shuddered through the mess while he decided what to do next. For a split-second, he looked at Chief with glassy, remorseful eyes. It had happened so quickly, this, like a child throwing a stone and breaking a window. An accident, almost. But then, without further deliberation, he brought his tremendous fist down atop Gilroy's hat, and there was a cracking sound as the man's teeth crashed together and broke to pieces inside his mouth. Gilroy made an *ullllggg* sound from his chest, and his legs gave out beneath him as he slumped to the floor.

Later, one of the men would remark that he'd looked like Charlie Chaplin might if Betty Compson had walked by with her lipstick fresh and her blouse undone.

The typical thing after a fight was to laugh and hoot, to slap the victor on the back and offer a shot of whiskey from an illicit flask; normally, they would help the loser to his feet, congratulate him on not dying, offer *him* a shot of whiskey, too, to help still any rung bells. Not today. It was clear this fight was different. Somebody held a drink out to Standard, which he declined with a shake of the head. The rest of them stayed quiet, frightened by what they'd just witnessed, and they looked at the new man with wide eyes and a sort of terrified respect. They left Gilroy, whom nobody really liked anyway, on the floor.

Standard went over to the biscuits he'd dumped on the ground and began tossing them back onto the tray.

"Bring them over here," Gary Childress called out. "I'll still eat them motherfuckers."

THEY WERE STANDING IN THE SILENCE left behind by the whistling when Wallace Wilson pulled in with his team of mules to move Chief and his dogs back down the mountain. He was a forcibly ugly fellow of indeterminable age, with a freckled forehead and a significant overbite and a pair of flying nostrils like the wings of a bat. He had a distinctly country demeanor, a sort of cool nonchalance: when the men whistled their teasing come-hithers, he paid no attention other than to swipe away an imaginary insect and flex the ropey muscles in his arms. He wore a mustache and smoked a brown cigarillo that seemed never to draw down. Chief could see the outline of the package it came from in the chest pocket of his shirt.

"Pray grace for my tardiness," Wilson said, unlashing the mules from his cart, so they could get at a patch of new grass while he did his work. "Standing water in Mama's house. Up to your knees for two days now." His lips curled and uncurled around the cigarillo when he spoke.

"Good Christ," Chief said sharply. Now that his man was here, he wanted nothing more than to get on with getting home. "I hope it's gone down."

"Nope," Wilson said. "Still there. We slept on a bed of water last night, just—" and he crossed his arms and closed his eyes and pretended to be floating. He opened his eyes, removed the cigarillo, and smiled. His teeth jutted from his lips like corn kernels.

"I'm grateful for the attention in your time of need," Chief said, still conversing despite himself. Wilson was friendly, after all, if a little goofy; still, Chief's desire to leave out had only grown more urgent. The longer he stayed, the longer he knew he'd want to stay.

His men rested outside their tents watching Wilson load gear onto the cart. Gary Childress, who would that evening be moving into Chief's bigger hooch and assuming his supervisory duties, sat rubbing the dogs behind their ears. The men perched on damp stumps and mossy patches of rock with their hats in their laps or pushed high back on their foreheads, worrying about the whistling. They'd often sit together in the evenings and gotten drunk and talked about the ghosts they'd seen or heard or known about in their lives; this man had a specter in his grandmother's back yard, this one a poltergeist who delighted in striking his uncle's matches and tossing them onto the packed mud floor. A funny kid named Hutchins, dead now several years, had once joked that his mother was haunted by the spirit of an anxious letter carrier who seemed to know when his father left for work. When the pale postman was sure the coast was clear, it would drag his mother, who laughed when she was scared, into the cellar.

"What would they do in the cellar?" the men would ask.

"She always said she was shining his shoes."

And they would laugh maniacally, toss and fall about like drunken animals.

But now they knew for sure they'd been admonished, that Standard's ghost had returned to warn them from their old habits. Even in death, he was bigger than them. So they sat still, half-listening for Standard's little tune through the percussion of rain falling behind them in the woods. It was quiet work for some time: they sat whittling and chewing the grit from underneath their fingernails and watching Wallace Wilson load Chief's life onto his cart.

"Get a load of that," one of them said finally, and they turned as a group to where he'd pointed. There, far back in the woods and down the slope of the hill a ways, floated the rough pine box they all recognized as the one in which they'd buried the giant Clayton Standard.

"Bullshit," Gary Childress said, standing and peering through the trees. "We planted that box eight foot deep."

"Ten foot, probably," someone said.

"And piled high with rocks," another man said.

And yet there it was, swaying gently on the wake of the overburdened creek. It had likely been making its way toward them for several days while the snowmelt lifted it like a paper boat. Its lid had come askew, and its planks were brown and sodden, but it was without a doubt the casket that had once held the peculiar oaf's remains.

"Y'all boys go down there and hook it up," Chief said, surprised at the authority he'd managed to summon. "It can't just float around the holler all afternoon." He could feel a palsy in his hands, as though a current were charging through him.

The boy Glick, who'd slowly been forgiven and repatriated into their ranks, volunteered to be part of the team to wade out and fish the casket onto solid ground. He and a group of three other young lumberjacks, eager to do something unusual and thereby become part of a story that would be told for years, carried lengths of rope on their shoulders and iron log hooks in their hands and set off down the hill.

The men, of course, stood on dry ground above them, calling out ridiculous directions:

"Don't let 'er spin southward on ya, it's bad luck."

"The smell of death can make a man go blind!"

"That's the truth! Cover your mouth with your shirt!"

"If Mama's in that box, tell her Henry loves her very much!"

And so on.

The cluster of men approached the box in water to mid-thigh, holding their hands up like string puppets to keep the current from stripping their tools away and, Chief suspected, from freezing their peckers. A pair of them managed to flank the casket on the far side while the other two steadied it nearby, and they attached their hooks to its various crevices and hinges and slung their ropes over their shoulders and began to pull. At first, it seemed easy going, but now and then the current shifted and the box dragged the boys from their centering, caused them to heel sideways—to the delight of the men watching, who groaned comically when they fell off course and cheered and clapped when they managed to right themselves. Chief found the operation too harrowing to watch: inside that coffin was four hundred pounds of waterlogged flesh, frozen and thawed again, likely bloated beyond recognition, not to mention the mound of silt that was sure to have filtered in, the leaves and pebbles and other detritus that loves to fill the gaps of underwater vessels.

At length, they managed to haul the casket close enough to solid ground that it could rest on shore and not charge around the forest on its peculiar course. Chief took his hat off and stepped toward it. His men unconsciously split a gap for him to come through.

They'd carved Standard's name into the lid of the box, along with the date he was killed. Chief read it quietly and glanced at Glick, who stood to his knees in the ice-cold water, hunting for a decent draw of air and looking down at the casket as though there were something there he simply couldn't understand. Chief felt an immense sympathy for the boy, for not knowing what he'd done, for assuming—as was only right to assume—that a deathstrike to Clayton Standard would have meant little to anyone else on Earth. Here came a threat that the boy had the improbable ability to quiet, and he'd quieted it. It didn't have to be that simple for everyone, but it was inevitably that simple for Glick.

"Clayton Standard?" someone behind Chief said, a small voice with a thick holler accent. Chief turned to see Wallace Wilson, the muleteer, standing just over his shoulder. "Hell," Wilson said, chewing the butt end of his cigarillo, "ain't nobody heard from that old boy in years."

THE YEAR AFTER STANDARD APPEARED, a decree came from Baltimore. Company bosses—men in topcoats and round spectacles, hand-wringers, doomsday prophets—had grown convinced that the coming winter would be a terrible one; of special concern, the letter noted, was the risk of gale-force winds and blinding snow that would make work in the timber fields all but impossible. "It is hoped," the letter said, "that your company will redouble its harvesting efforts in the fall months, that we may mitigate any reduction in revenue that would be caused by the uncommonly harsh period that seems destined to follow."

Chief had read the letter aloud at breakfast mess and the men laughed with their mouths full of food. There was much that deserved their ridicule. "Redoubling harvesting efforts" was simple enough, they joked; simply redouble the number of sawyers in camp. To the man who sat at the bottom looking up, "reduction in revenue" was nothing but corporate blabbermouthing (Chief, though, knew coded language for *layoffs* when he heard it; he kept his interpretation to himself, fearful always of pay-based mutiny). That word "destined" was the one that really got their blood boiling: what did these cocksuckers in Baltimore know about *destiny*? How, indeed, did licking the nib of a pen and endorsing the back of a check qualify one to pontificate on *anything*? How did securing the polished bone buttons of one's woolen waistcoat and combing one's hair to a spit-shine prepare an intimate knowledge of the moods of the Fates? Come to the forest, the lumberjacks thought, and watch a man's head be swiped from his shoulders at the arc of a falling limb; watch a fellow have his legs sawn off by the flash-bulb recoil of a choker chain snapped in twain; stand a nighttime shift in ankle deep mud with a rifle on your shoulder, searching between plum-sized raindrops for the glinting eyes of the mountain lion who's stalked your camp for over a fortnight... then, perhaps, we shall talk about what we mean when we speak of *destiny*. Chief's men knew destiny at close range and did not see it as something to be heralded or sought after. To them, it made more sense to avoid their *destiny* with all the energy they could muster.

He did not read aloud the part of the letter that threatened his job should the company's work be found unsatisfactory. He did not see it as any of the men's concern and did not want them to suppose they were being asked to speed their efforts on his personal behalf. He would either find a way or he would not. If there came a reward, he would tip the cup, so that all dogs might have a drink. If there came a punishment, he would bear it solely upon his own shoulders.

Of course, they already knew that any increase in output for the fall would never be rewarded with downtime in winter; should the weather *not* turn in November, should forecasts of belligerent blizzards, of frozen damnation and apocalyptic windstorms, turn out to be so much hogwallop, those fat city bastards in Baltimore would doubtless compose a *new* letter, one that praised God for his mercy in the time of their greatest need—forgetting, as they watched their butlers polish the silver, as they took cognac in their parlors with ambassadors from tropical nations, as their white-stockinged heirs ran ragged circles around their feet like excited little dogs, that their prayers had been answered not by the will of God but by the skill of a hundred coarse, hollow men on a hillside in the deep Appalachian forest, men who swung axes and pulled saws and spent their drunken weekends asleep on the sweat-slicked bellies of cheap country whores. There would be no further thought of these men from Baltimore. Baltimore may have been where the paychecks came from, but right there on the hillside is where the real men worked.

"So, we'll redouble our efforts, I guess," Chief said, folding the letter and tucking it into his pocket. The men went on eating. They were the sort of men who knew their lot in life, which was not to argue with Baltimore.

When they were finished with their meals, though, they took the pinches of food they'd set aside for Atropos and stuffed them into their mouths. If they were going to work harder, their bellies would need to be full.

It was from Wallace Wilson that they received Clayton Standard's history. Born in the town of Minnow ("famous for fishing," Wilson said) to Benjamin Standard, the county's worst drunk, and his wife, Hettie, a schoolteacher, Clayton was destined for shunning: the shining gap between his lip and his nose had turned most everyone away, even his own kin, and Hettie's embarrassment of it and her weariness in explaining it to every ignorant passer-by had eventually driven her to remove the baby from public altogether. The family kept a homestead in some woods that could not be seen from any road; it was here that Hettie raised the boy while Benjamin slept off his liquor with his head in the leaves. When she taught, Hettie was forced to pass the boy off to his father, which meant Clayton was left to raise himself. "Under the circumstances," the boy Wallace said, "I'd say he did okay at it." He could bait a hook when he was two years old and knock an arrow when he was three. By five, he'd taught himself to field-dress a deer and could salt-preserve its meat for wintertime without the help of anyone whatsoever.

Though Benjamin Standard was ill with drink, Wallace said, he was not by nature a mean or unloving man, and one day when Clayton was six, Benjamin came stumbling into the cabin, where Clayton and Hettie were reading *Treasure Island* by the mantel, with good news.

"I've won a bet," he announced, drawing little more than a glance from the boy or his mother. He huffed and cocked his head sideways. "Did you hear me, woman?"

"I heard you," Hettie said softly, and turned back to her son. "You know how little impressed I am with gambling."

"You'll be impressed on this occasion," Benjamin said. He reached into his frayed waistcoat and removed a slip of folded paper. "'This is to certify,'" he began slowly. He squinted at the paper in the dim light. "That is to say, 'This is to certify that one Benjamin Standard,' yes, yes, 'during a game of stud, has acquired the services of myself, M. Farraday, dentist,'—a fellow I sometimes play cards with, that is—'of the nature of attending to his son, one Clayton Benjamin Standard, suffering since childbirth from hare-lip, for surgical rectification of said disorder. Debt payable in the order designed by Mr. Standard. Signed, M. Farraday,' and so on."

It was the clearest declaration of love that Benjamin Standard had ever uttered. He'd been offered his pick of a seven-year-old Saddlebred mare, the deed to a hunting cabin outside Holmesdale, or the complicated procedure of correcting his son's deformity. He'd decided on the latter, he claimed, "with absolutely no deliberation necessary." He and the dentist Farraday had agreed on a date of the following Saturday for the surgery.

"It's said Hettie Standard looked on her baby boy without blinking for the next eight days," Wallace Wilson said, chomping on the butt of his cigarillo, clearly happy for the audience of lumberjacks gathering around him. "And when that Saturday morning finally came, she insisted on Farraday's completing the surgery while she held the boy in her lap."

Which is, more or less, what happened. Standard was larger than a regular six-year-old, though, far larger, and his squirming and writhing therefore much harder to contain; these were the infant days of anesthesia, mind, and so even the mask of chloroform Farraday offered the child did not sufficiently contain his protestations. Instead, it made him drunk with a bewildered sort of anger: he floated in and out of consciousness as the doctor proceeded with his work, startling now and then from his dreams in a state of flailing incomprehension, as though he'd awoken to find he'd been dropped into a pit of vipers.

After an hour of strain, Farraday clipped the final stitch and backed away from the chair, his breathing labored and his hands raised in a posture of self-defense. The boy slumped against his mother's breast, and they lay there together, exhausted. She arched her neck to look at his face, which was coated ear-to-ear with a film of browning blood; the lip, though, had clearly been fused, and for this, she could be nothing but grateful.

THE RESULTING SEASON—the season of redoubled effort, as it were—became different things at once.

To begin with, it was hectic. To make for quicker work, and possibly to prove his worth as a leader of men, Gary Childress suggested to Chief that they split their ranks into four groups (Childress called them "clans," for some reason or other) and disperse to different sites across the hillside. The company had not seen fit to provide more men, but the suits in Baltimore *had* managed to scrape together several old tractors—a pair of Model Ts and a Wallis—for skidding. They came on the Summersville train and the men drew straws to see who would go down and retrieve them. After a day of waiting, they heard a rumbling from down the road, and they gathered outside the mess to watch the tractors pull in, their drivers smiling and sweat-streaked like boys come in from a football game. They waved grand gestures with their hats and drove with their feet jutting out from the tractor flanks. They were like cowboys showing off atop beaten-down, undersized nags.

The tractors, along with the one they already had, allowed each clan to have its own heavy equipment (if these pathetic beasts deserved such a title), and they all had a team of horses, and twenty or thirty men working in pairs. The greenhorns were strategically split among the clans to ensure no single group suffered from an abundance of inexperience. Chief had drawn a crude map of the acreage and assigned the clans their sections. He tried to start each group on land of equally challenging topography, lest he have a four-state civil war on his hands at the end of the first day. In this, his success could only go so far.

Standard was assigned to Clan Three, and though it was unclear to Chief how the men of Clan Three felt about it, Standard quickly and without much resistance became the leader of his crew: it was true that his skill had accumulated quickly, but moreover, he was not afraid to fight any man who claimed it hadn't. He would drive his men hard, push them from one tree to the next, orchestrating teams like a child arranging toy soldiers in a backyard battlefield. This was not easy for them to accept, but Chief had instituted an incentive program for the team that felled the most timber in any given week: an extra dollar in each man's pocket to take with him to Summersville and do with as he pleased. An extra dollar was a fortune, not for what it was but for what the clever operator could turn it into: five more beers, four more shots of whiskey, an extra half-hour with one of the less-practiced girls. An extra dollar could sustain a man for the remainder of his evening, if he used it wisely. Standard's men looked at their overgrown, foul-tempered commandant and knew the supplemental income was as good as theirs. All they'd have to do was nearly die to get it.

If the season was frenzied, it was also deadly. Thanks to heated competition drummed up by the clan system and Chief's new incentive program, crews began making careless mistakes that cost fingers and time and, in four cases over the course of a single month, lives:

Coot Devereaux, a French-Canadian transplant whose father, grandfather, and great-grandfather had all been timbermen, had his feet jammed deep in the chainery of a go-devil while he connected a pair of logs to the sled and laughed at what an inopportune time it would be for the horses to take off. Then his clan's Wallis backfired, and the team *did* take off, and in a matter of a couple minutes, Devereaux was dragged to kingdom come and the logs he'd been fastening had rolled nearly halfway down a hundred-foot embankment. They found his body back in the woods, still connected to the horses, who'd come upon a patch from which to graze and stopped in their panic, uncaring of the loose rig of chains and hooks they'd been hauling behind them. Devereaux's skin was shredded away from the bone across his hands and cheeks and the sides of his belly, and there was a bloody dent in his forehead where the men guessed he'd passed over a rock and his lights had been permanently knocked out.

John Lyles had been too eager to pump a steam donkey, and when he fell into its gears, his arm was pulled off at the shoulder. He bled out belly-down on the ground, lapping at a dry pile of dirt and sawdust with his tongue. He died before anyone noticed he was there.

Arthur Gilchrist went the old-fashioned way: in his hurry to get somewhere else, he passed behind a man swinging a maul and neglected to announce his whereabouts. The broad side of the maul caught Gilchrist in the temple, and he fell flat on his back and simply never sat up again.

Then there was Majer Maurenbrecher, the German, a greenhorn who'd found his way to Appalachia on a steamer from New Orleans, where he'd made money for a while by painting his face like a jack-o-lantern and juggling beer bottles in the French Quarter. Maurenbrecher hadn't even been in the field when he caught his end. Some of the clans endorsed an unofficial policy of skipping meals in the mess on certain nights in order to get more work done, and on these nights, the men were largely left on their own to scrounge up their dinners. Maurenbrecher had had the good fortune to shoot a squirrel during the day, and that evening, he set it on a makeshift spit outside his hooch and lay down for a nap. The squirrel, grown fat in scavenging for the upcoming winter, began to drip heavy bulbs of grease into Maurenbrecher's embers; eventually the flames grew too large, the spit caved under, the animal fell in, and the erupting sparks lit the tips of his tent flaps. When he finally woke, he was surrounded by flame, and in his panic, he stood straight up and found himself wrapped in burning canvas. Wearing this blanket of fire around his head and shoulders and screaming like a terrified pig, Maurenbrecher stumbled into the camp, tripping and swaying, until a couple of men tackled him and began to beat at the tent with their hats and bare hands. More men showed up with buckets of water and dumped it over the whole writhing mess, and by the time Maurenbrecher was done sizzling, his screaming had stopped. When they peeled what was left of his hooch away, they could barely recognize as human the thing that lay there, smoking, its skin shiny and buckled like bacon in the pan.

It should be said that the violence of that season would have been worse if not for Clayton Standard. Take the story of a boy named Harris, who'd gone to Summersville on the train one weekend and spent his first few hours in town getting drunk in a local speakeasy. When he emerged in an alleyway, looking for a place to drain his bladder, it was still daylight; in fact, it was not yet noon, and here the boy Harris was, wobbling in his boots, leaning on a wall in a town he did not know, puking, groaning, grunting. He righted himself and marched twenty yards one way, did not emerge onto any street, about-faced, and marched twenty yards back. He found himself hopelessly lost, stuck in a strange subterranean tunnel with no entry and no exit. He thought he'd go back into the speakeasy, find his friends, maybe sleep off his liquor in the corner until somebody dragged him to a bed somewhere. So, he grabbed the door handle and flung it open and stepped in. He was struck by the newfound cleanliness of the bar, by its vitamin smell and lack of patronage. The room before him was filled with bright powdery light, "like Heaven," he'd later recall, though there had, of course, been no such light in the speakeasy, which was actually a dank and foreboding cave and full of the heaving bodies of sweating sacks of shit. Here, though, Harris looked around and saw rows of shelves neatly done-up with glass bottles and paper sacks. On the counter, a basket of penny candies. He'd wandered into the back door of a pharmacist's thinking it was a drinkery, and, seeing no one around to stop him from anything, his eyes widened with sudden possibility. In a fit of mania, he stuffed the pockets of his overcoat with tinctures of bromide, bottles of heroin hydrochloride, and packets of cocaine tabs. Unable to comprehend his good luck but fearing it may run short, he took one more sweeping glance through the store and snatched up a handful of the candy and walked right back out the door through which he'd entered. (It would be established, through a subsequent investigation of the robbery, that the pharmacy owner's son, a hapless sixteen-year-old who'd fallen in love with the Cherokee girl working at the laundry across the street, had gone out to bring her some chocolate and neglected to lock the door behind him; he'd been away for approximately seven minutes. Thus, Harris's feckless good fortune would profit.)

Harris brought his stash back to camp, of course, and soon enough he and several other greenhorns found themselves directed by demons they didn't understand and had little control over. The profit dissipated quickly. They carried their soggy weight into the fields, stumbling over the toes of their boots and sleeping with their backs against root balls. Their comrades, neither stupid nor blind, gave them hell for it: to be under the persistent influence of a little something here and there was to be expected, a man's tolerance for it almost admired, but to allow oneself to fall so deeply into its throes was amateurish, and they had little respect for amateurs. Amateurs got men killed. The stuporous clump of boys would therefore stand off to the side and have insults hurled at them, find themselves pelted with hard little clods of mud and tripped from underneath with the sweeping leg of a passing sawyer. Now and then, someone would take a swing with his fist.

"Get your minds right, boys," a man would say.

"I've a mind to kill all four of you," a man would say.

"I am *absolutely* going to kill all four of you," a man would say.

After several days of this, the men were relegated to a small section to clear limb shoots from castaway logs that would be used for firewood. They spent all day in their little cordoned area, trusted only with hatchets for shaving away little branches, picking at themselves and grunting, until one day Harris heard an incredible *whooshing* sound and then the frantic calls of men somewhere in the woods, and he looked up to see the top of a giant hickory arcing above him, crashing headlong through the canopy, and even in his sublime mental state, he could calculate that it would strike him and his friends and all of them would die more or less instantly. He was simply too high to say anything about it.

Those four men *would* have died instantly if not for Clayton Standard, who'd seen the mistake as it was happening and taken off running. In the five seconds between the fatal blow being struck to the tree and the tree's fatal blow being struck to Harris and his friends, Standard positioned himself at a spot he figured to be halfway between stump and victims and waited.

His men yelled at him from all directions—*Get your ass clear, Standard!; you're a dead man, Standard!*—but just before the tree struck him in the head, Standard crouched and raised his hands and simply... caught it. He let loose a terrific grunt and allowed the tree's massive weight to slap his hands and buckle his elbows, and then he sank low onto one knee and settled with his new burden into the tacky mud of the forest floor. Men came running to help him, sawyers with their blades who cut the tree midway down its trunk and thereby cut its weight in half and, with a single mighty push, Standard heaved the tree away from himself. It shook the ground so hard the men's toes vibrated in their boots.

"I ain't never seen nothin!" Harris shouted behind him. The intoxicated boy ran toward Standard, clapping his hands like a child. "Holy God, I ain't never seen nothin!"

Standard finished dusting himself off and turned just before Harris reached him and delivered a straight jab into the meat of the boy's mouth, which the boy sort of hung upon for a second like a limp windsock, so deep was the impression that Standard's fist made in his face. His teeth cut gashes into the back of Standard's hand. Then he dropped to the ground, a hunk of cold meat, and Standard walked away from him to rejoin his crew.

After that, every man in camp knew he owed Clayton Standard a small debt of gratitude. Not only the four men whose lives he'd saved, the irresponsible morons in their holding pen, but the rest of them too. From now on, they could work knowing Clayton Standard would be there to protect them in his blunt and brutal way, like a rusty piece of armor across their shoulders, a dented helmet to cover their heads.

In the fall of Clayton's seventh year, Benjamin Standard disappeared. It was a foregone conclusion that he would one day go; still, nobody, with the possible exception of Hettie, had expected he'd go without saying goodbye to his only son.

"How I heard it," Wilson said, "there had been a card game, a round of faro, which Benjamin had never favored but would play if it was the only thing around." A simple, friendly card game, though in those days, anything simple and friendly could turn mighty complex in two shakes of a dead lamb's tail (as Wilson put it); this game of faro would turn out to be no different.

Benjamin hiked his britches and settled onto a stool. There were a couple other men around him, along with the dealer and landlord, a chompy old fellow named Beauregard Bingham who suffered from recurrent Bell's palsy, which made his right eye leak and the corner of his lip tremble. Beau, the men called him, sometimes Weepin' Beau, sometimes just Weepy. Beau was the bartender and the banker and the town head-shrinker, the guy the younger fellows went to for advice— on women, money, farming, hair pomade—you name it, Beauregard Bingham was the local authority. And as Benjamin Standard sat down and began to stack his chips, he understood quickly that Beau had gotten himself into an exchange with a young man Benjamin recognized from neighboring Flat Rock: Elroy Halbfinger, who just happened to be the undersheriff of Lancaster County ("which ain't saying much... his daddy was the sheriff," Wilson said). Halbfinger preferred to wear his badge at all times, even at a faro table, where it was at best inappropriate and at worst threatened his very life and the lives of everyone around him.

Benjamin glanced sideways at a display case that rested against a wall. He could see part of himself in it, and parts of the other players—their dusty bottoms hanging off the backs of their stools, the pinches of shirt pulling away from their waistbands. Inside the case were the type of knickknacks one's grandmother might collect: bells and spoons and shells from some faraway shoreline. An antique book or two. A pair of silver rings.

"Goddamn, Weepy," Halbfinger was saying, just as Benjamin Standard was getting himself settled. "The woman's a twelve on a ten scale. Skin's as slick as a brook trout, a fine mess of yellow hair, and a fire in that belly like nothin I've ever known before. Sweet Jesus."

"You want to shut up now, Halbfinger?" Beau said. He gave Benjamin a look that seemed sort of apologetic.

"Blows like a gale wind," the undersheriff said. "Thirsty as all get-out." He made lapping, fish-like sounds with his lips.

"Halbfinger, goddammit," Beau said. "Shut your trap and place a bet."

Halbfinger glanced at Benjamin and chuckled. "What's the big deal? It's a game of cards, for fuck's sake. A man can say what he wants at a game of cards, can't he?"

Beau pointed at Benjamin. "Place a bet?"

Benjamin placed a chip on a corner and waited for the loser. It was a six.

"Shit," Halbfinger said. He'd lost the hand, so he sat back and sipped his whiskey.

The winner was a queen. Beau pushed a few chips toward Benjamin.

"She won't let me in the cabin, on account of her kid," Halbfinger said, casting his eyes to the corner of the room and talking to no one in particular. "So we've been going out to the shithouse."

"Halb—" Beau started, but Halbfinger cut him off.

"The kid's a half-wit of some kind."

"Excuse me, gentlemen," the older fellow at the end of the table said. He coughed loudly and pocketed his chips and adjusted his dusty waistcoat. "Best be gettin home to the girls."

"Anyway, we don't fuck *inside* the shithouse," Halbfinger said, and turned to look directly at Benjamin. "Usually, I bend her over against the back wall there. That way she got somethin to push against."

Benjamin was in no mood to hear about Undersheriff Halbfinger's sexual transgressions, but neither was he in much of a position to shut the man up: Benjamin was a drunk, an on-again, off-again drifter, a casual acquaintance of many of the county's more practiced criminals (if not a very practiced one himself); it would not be unusual for one of his bootlegger friends to be sleeping in his barn, and he occasionally rented the sanctity of the hills above his homestead for the private and untormented construction of corn-liquor stills. He couldn't be sure Halbfinger knew who he was, but it was prudent to operate under the assumption that he did.

They played several hands over which Halbfinger proved himself an incompetent gambler; he bet the corners far too often and played his copper when there was no benefit.

He challenged Beau over and again by putting money on the high card—a fifty-fifty chance every time. Even the dumbest card players knew that a toss-up tilted toward the house. Benjamin sat for an hour watching his own stack slowly grow while Halbfinger's wilted like a plucked flower.

For his part, Halbfinger seemed not to mind. He was rambling on and on about this woman: her yellow hair, her warm cocoon, her knobby knees crumby and flushed when she rose from the ground. Benjamin assumed he was talking about some whore he knew from Flat Rock, somebody young and stupid and easy to disadvantage.

"I think we might be in love," Halbfinger said finally, and it was the look Beau accidentally gave Benjamin then, a horrible look of sorrow, that settled the thing into place. Benjamin felt a stone in his gut and turned to the undersheriff, who was listing a little in his chair from drink and smiling like an asshole.

"You been talking this broad up somethin heavy," Benjamin said. "It occurs to me I should maybe meet her too. How much she been chargin you?"

Halbfinger turned his smile toward Benjamin. "She don't usually name a price," he said. "But I'm a nice guy, you know. I throw her a buck or two."

"And where'd you say she's living?"

Halbfinger's smile crossed his whole face, and his big, crooked teeth emerged like a skeleton being born. *Your place,* he said, and barked out a laugh.

The ensuing fistfight was brutal and necessary. Benjamin Standard stood quickly and raked his fingernails down Undersheriff Halbfinger's face from forehead to chin, leaving the man temporarily blinded and with red trails like chigger marks on his cheeks. Plump droplets of blood began to bulge where Standard had broken the skin. Halbfinger took a swing, but he was drunk and his eyes had filled with blood, and he couldn't see what he was aiming for. Benjamin ducked it easily and came underneath to take a shot at his ribs, which landed with a crack and doubled the undersheriff over. He stood there, creased and moaning, while Benjamin took either side of his head in his hands and held it in place while he brought his knee up sharply to meet Halbfinger's face. He could feel the meat of Halbfinger's nose mashing against his leg and heard the pop of cartilage snapping out of place, and when Benjamin let go of his head, Halbfinger fell back onto the floor, kicking up a cloud of dust in the midday sun and rattling the knickknacks in Weepy's display case.

Bingham stood over the heap of Elroy Halbfinger, watching the young man's eyelids flutter. The whole thing had taken thirty seconds.

"You know you can't stay here," he said.

"Tell me something new, old fella," Benjamin said.

"Hold up," Gary Childress said. He'd been sitting on the sodden edge of Clayton Standard's coffin, listening to Wallace Wilson's story. "I figured this Halbfinger stud was fixin to show Standard what's what.

"He sure didn't do that," Wilson said.

"But you said Benjamin Standard went quick."

"The minute a man's heart stops beating and the minute he dies don't have to be the same minute," Wilson said. "Hell, Benjamin Standard lived another seventeen years. Matter of fact, he just died—for real *died,* that is—not too long ago, 'bout over thataway." He turned to point through the woods in a westward direction.

The men glanced at each other with looks of confusion.

"Lookit," Wallace Wilson said. "Benjamin Standard never got to see his wife or his boy ever again. He couldn't show his face nowhere around for the rest of his life. He never made another honest nickel. What few friends he had were done with him for good; they was all crooks and cheats, and he was more heat than ever after he got done beatin hell out of a cop. Them Halbfinger boys would be on the hunt til they couldn't walk no more."

"Livin dead man," the boy Glick said.

"Thereabouts," Wilson said.

On the evening of that day when Clayton Standard caught the hickory tree in his bare hands, Chief called him to a table in the empty, after-supper mess with a mind to berate him in private. *You're worth forty of those type of men,* he was thinking. *If those fellas were hell-bent on getting themselves killed, you should have let them. I can't lose you.* And actually, those four words had circled in his head like a mantra from the minute he heard about what Standard had done. *I can't lose you. I can't lose you.* More than anything else, they confused him: he'd never felt so strongly about any man, not even Gary Childress, who he'd worked alongside for nearly fifteen years and who was probably his best friend.

"Chief?" Standard called from outside the screen door. "You in?"

"Come on in," Chief said, his anger already fading.

Standard's hands were wrapped in several layers of pus-soaked gauze. Perkins, the camp medic, had removed several dozen penknife-sized slivers of wood from the meat of Standard's paws and tightened bandages around the raw spots where his fingernails were peeled away. The skin on Standard's palms had been shaved off by tree bark just as though he'd taken a sharp blade to it. When Perkins washed the blood away with saline, he said he could see the wriggling ends of Standard's veins under the new skin. He'd coated the friction burns with Tannafax and bound the hands and patted Standard on the shoulder without saying anything else.

When Standard came in, his big body looked somehow smaller. He settled his weight onto a bench across from Chief and slumped his shoulders.

"Jesus Christmas," Chief said, looking at the hands Standard held in his lap like a scolded schoolboy.

"Well," Standard said.

"How long are you off for?"

"Few days."

"Give em here."

Standard extended his hands so that Chief could hold them. The foreman turned them over gently, inspecting the damage. The gauze was wrapped thick as boxing gloves. Standard winced whenever Chief touched a raw spot.

"We're fortunate to have Perkins," Chief said.

Standard didn't say anything. He looked over his shoulder into the mess kitchen, where two men were scrubbing supper dishes and singing a song he recognized but couldn't make out the words to. He drew his hands back from Chief's lap and sat quietly.

"I just hadn't gotten around to firing them boys yet," Chief said, meaning Harris and his crew.

"Well," Standard said.

"There's plenty boys want to take their spots."

"They don't need firing," Standard said. "They need work. They need somebody smarter than they are to stay on top of them. Somebody with balls enough to come down hard when they fuck up."

Chief didn't argue because he knew what Standard was saying, and he knew it was right.

"You don't think I got the guts," Chief said.

"Well, now that you say so," Standard said, "I don't suppose there's such a huge gap between that and the truth."

Chief sighed. "I guess I just never felt the need."

Standard looked over Chief's shoulder and into the kitchen. The pot scrubbers had noticed them and periodically poked their heads out to eavesdrop.

"You never been with a woman, have you?" Standard said.

Chief huffed and leaned back. "Course I have," he said. He looked at Standard with heavy eyes. "I been with my share. Well, I don't go around publicizing myself like some men do."

"And did it agree with you?"

"Did it agree with me?"

Standard leaned forward, eagerly, like a hunter watching a snare. "Did you *like* it?"

Chief struggled to answer. What did it mean to *like* something? What did it have to do with anything if you did?

"I probably haven't done anything I liked in all my life," he said.

"You got them books under your pillow," Standard said. "Don't you like those?"

Chief felt his face redden. "What do you know about it?"

"Enough."

"My mother's a reader," Chief admitted. "I get it from her."

"Ain't no shame in learning something you didn't know before," Standard said. He leaned forward a little more. His eyes were blue as lake water.

Chief adjusted himself and wiped his sweaty palms on his legs. How had he gotten here?

WITH HIS FATHER'S SMALL ECONOMY run off and the force of his own physical appearance now tempered thanks to the dentist Farraday, young Clayton struck off into the world to find work and help his mother keep their home. Though he was but seven years old by then, he was broad in the shoulders and had a stout, powerful gut—"like a grizzly," Wallace Wilson said—and quickly found work unloading pallets at Mandell's Seed Service on Gauley Street in Minnow, a job he was particularly well-suited for, both in strength and in his boundless, fiery sort of energy. The store's owners, brothers Glen and Thomas Mandell, men who had the bodies and facial expressions of young cattle, would stand on the wooden loading dock and smoke cigars and watch the boy at work. They joked that Standard would grow up bent double, that he'd be forced to walk at a right angle for the rest of his days thanks to them. When Standard would finally acknowledge them and stand up purposefully, straight as an Indian arrow and with a naive look of pride on his face, they would be delighted. To them, the more warped the boy became, the more hilarious it would be.

"Sure, you look sturdy now, kid," Thomas Mandell would say, "but wait til you're thirty. Thirty'll wipe that shiteatin grin right off your ugly little face." And the brothers would laugh and puff cigar smoke out of their noses and through the hair of their bushy thirty-year-old mustaches.

Among the Mandell brothers' favorite targets was Benjamin Standard, whom they called a worthless pile of shit, not worth the paper his birth certificate was written upon. Church-going men themselves, the Mandells laid siege to Benjamin's entire composition: his addictions and lusts, his terrible fortune at cards.

"I once saw Benjamin Standard lose a hundred dollars to a nun and a man with a carrot in his ass," Thomas Mandell said. Clayton stood below him, tossing seedbags onto a pallet. "I heard he slept in the toilet out back of Jeremiah Grisham's bar for three days before Grisham caught him trying to stuff a straw mattress inside," Glen said.

Whenever he heard his father's name, Clayton had a habit of touching the thick scar tissue at the base of his nose—his only reminder that being the son of Benjamin Standard had not been a total waste of effort. In truth, the Mandells were right; Benjamin Standard *had* been useless. Clayton had never gotten a single birthday present from his father, not a piece of candy nor a paperback novel. He doubted that his father even knew when his birthday was. He'd often stumbled across the old man sleeping outside, head on a log or a pile of rolled moss, and he'd certainly not been blessed with the childhood lesson of warmth between parents. Still, on one important occasion when Benjamin Standard could have enriched himself generously, at one of the rare times when his luck had come to the table alongside him, Benjamin had chosen the social survival of his son over the health of his own financial situation. This simple fact did not erase his hatred of the man, but in Clayton's view, it gave the son sole privilege in speaking ill against the father.

"Fuck the bunch of you," Standard would say, but under his breath, so the brothers couldn't hear. He fantasized about breaking a fifty-pound feedbag over Thomas Mandell's head. Standard knew just which words Thomas would use as he came to: *You're nothin but meat, boy. Shit with eyes. Build them muscles up, 'cause them brains won't help you.* The men were often mean like this, especially when times were slow at the shop and they'd been drinking behind the counter. They liked to make sure Standard knew his place in the world. They loved reminding him that his daddy was a good-for-nothin, and that his mama was a whore. So taken were they by Standard's physicality, though, that they often forgot he wasn't the same age as them, that he was, in fact, barely old enough to tie his own boots, that the careless words that came out of their mouths might have the power to ruin him for the rest of his life.

"Not that Standard had any intention of letting that happen," Wallace Wilson said. Wilson had gotten the full attention of the timbermen with his story of the fight between Benjamin Standard and Elroy Halbfinger, and there were now sixty or more men standing around Clayton Standard's coffin, which Wilson had climbed atop to use as a sort of flimsy stage from which to tell his story. "He worked for the Mandell boys for a couple more years until he couldn't take it no more. Then one night when he was nine years old, he broke into the feed store and cleaned the place out. He'd watched them Mandell boys open the safe so many times, he could do it with his eyes shut. He took out the cash money and the change purse and left the safe hanging open. He brought the seed bags in from the storage shed and piled them in the middle of the store. Poured kerosene all over them and struck them afire. The blaze flattened the building. Wasn't nothing but a pile of pick-up sticks when it was over."

"Hell," Gary Childress said, "at least he got his pride back."

"Maybe," Wilson said.

"Them Mandell boys go after theirs?" someone shouted from the crowd.

"They'd have wanted to, I'm sure," Wilson said. "But first, they'd have to live through the night."

"I'VE BEEN RUNNING MOST OF MY LIFE,"
The boys in the kitchen seemed to be finishing
pots on iron hooks and brushing the tabletops
Their song had died to a murmur.

"I figured as much," Chief said.

"Haven't felt like I was at home since I was
said. He raised his gauzed hands and laughed.
things."

"You done a number."

Just as one of the boys glanced at them fr
reached his hand out quickly, impulsively, and
face, from temple to chin. Chief could smel
bandages. He could feel the dampness from
could smell the iron in Clayton Standard's bl

"You know you have to leave here," Stand

Chief sat without saying anything. The
was still on his skin.

"I'll leave with you," Standard said. "I
away."

Chief looked at his feet. "I don't know,"

"You don't gotta know. I'll do the know

"Clayton," Chief said. He raised his h
room. "I ain't never had nothin but this."

Clayton Standard smiled. "Now you d

"THE MANDELLS SHARED a hundred-and-fifty-acre spread north of Minnow," the boy Wilson said. His voice had grown louder in the storytelling, his gestures more sweeping and confident. Chief watched as Wilson peddled his newfound wares: the life and times of Clayton Standard. He wondered how much of it Wilson knew to be true and how much of his story was only hillbilly claptrap, cast down through the leathery lips of some brother or uncle who claimed to have known Standard when they were mere runts coming up in the holler, who claimed to have been standing in the shadows when he burned Mandell's Seed to the ground, who claimed to have helped him dump the kerosene, to have spirited him away afterward on a borrowed nag. Chief had known so little about the dead man, and still he felt he'd known enough. Now and then, he turned his back to the story because of how unlikely it seemed.

"The Mandell homesteads were scattered across a fine stretch of timber," Wilson went on. "Nice houses they'd built off the same plans, water closets, and indoor cookstoves. Houses for families. Dogs. Barn cats running around in the yard. Each brother kept a chicken coop in his field. And the land up there? Incredible! You could turn around southward from anywhere and see clear to Minnow, clear to Wolf Hollow, even, away out on the Elkhorn River. I've been out thataway a few times, got a few customers out there myself. When there ain't no clouds at night, the moon'll light that part of the country up just as though it were lunchtime. That's the way it was on the night Clayton Standard went out avengin. Bright as day, though it was well past midnight.

"The way I heard it is that he snuck into Thomas Mandell's barn with a mind to find something he could use to slit the fat man's throat. He rummaged around a bit and come up with an old curry comb what was so rusty and dull, it wouldn'ta broken a man's skin if he was fresh outta the bath. He slipped it in his back pocket, anyway. Then he came across a set of sheep shears, the old spring-loaded kind, oiled and sharpened down to a fine split. He took them outside and tested them on the necks of some sunflowers and boy, their blades musta sparkled in the moonlight. Whack! Whack! He cut the heads offa all them sunflowers, what Thomas Mandell's daughter, Sarah, had planted in the springtime. It came out later she'd given them all their own names—Lillian, Gwendolyn, Harriet, and whatnot. But Clayton Standard killed each and ever one of em right there and left em dead in the grass.

"It's said there was a lantern still burning in the house, or else it had been lit while he was in the barn; I heard it both ways. The old boy crept up to the window and peered inside and saw Thomas Mandell's wife, Bernadette, who is a chubby woman and pleasant enough to look at, standing in the middle of the room, very still like, staring at nothing at all. As though she'd frozen in place. Of course, she wasn't looking, you understand, but *listening*.

"It hadn't occurred to Clayton that anybody other than Thomas Mandell would be inside the house. He hadn't counted on a family because in all his days working at the seed supply, he'd never once heard mention of any of the men's wives, nor of their children. In his mind, the Mandells were drunken stags who went home after work and stripped naked and drank whiskey and slept in heaps on the floor. But when he looked through the window, he realized he'd been wrong. He saw a clean, well-kempt home, a comely woman in her nightgown, a spinet piano against the wall. He could hear dogs yelping in the distance, probably from Glen's house."

he wasn't the same age as them, that he was, in fact, barely old enough to tie his own boots, that the careless words that came out of their mouths might have the power to ruin him for the rest of his life.

"Not that Standard had any intention of letting that happen," Wallace Wilson said. Wilson had gotten the full attention of the timbermen with his story of the fight between Benjamin Standard and Elroy Halbfinger, and there were now sixty or more men standing around Clayton Standard's coffin, which Wilson had climbed atop to use as a sort of flimsy stage from which to tell his story. "He worked for the Mandell boys for a couple more years until he couldn't take it no more. Then one night when he was nine years old, he broke into the feed store and cleaned the place out. He'd watched them Mandell boys open the safe so many times, he could do it with his eyes shut. He took out the cash money and the change purse and left the safe hanging open. He brought the seed bags in from the storage shed and piled them in the middle of the store. Poured kerosene all over them and struck them afire. The blaze flattened the building. Wasn't nothing but a pile of pick-up sticks when it was over."

"Hell," Gary Childress said, "at least he got his pride back."

"Maybe," Wilson said.

"Them Mandell boys go after theirs?" someone shouted from the crowd.

"They'd have wanted to, I'm sure," Wilson said. "But first, they'd have to live through the night."

"I'VE BEEN RUNNING MOST OF MY LIFE," Clayton Standard said. The boys in the kitchen seemed to be finishing up. They were hanging pots on iron hooks and brushing the tabletops with corn-straw brooms. Their song had died to a murmur.

"I figured as much," Chief said.

"Haven't felt like I was at home since I was nine years old," Standard said. He raised his gauzed hands and laughed. "Look at these goddamn things."

"You done a number."

Just as one of the boys glanced at them from the kitchen, Standard reached his hand out quickly, impulsively, and brushed it down Chief's face, from temple to chin. Chief could smell the Tannafax under the bandages. He could feel the dampness from the seeping wounds. He could smell the iron in Clayton Standard's blood.

"You know you have to leave here," Standard said.

Chief sat without saying anything. The weight of Standard's hand was still on his skin.

"I'll leave with you," Standard said. "I can show you how to run away."

Chief looked at his feet. "I don't know," he said.

"You don't gotta know. I'll do the knowin for you."

"Clayton," Chief said. He raised his hands and looked around the room. "I ain't never had nothin but this."

Clayton Standard smiled. "Now you do."

"THE MANDELLS SHARED a hundred-and-fifty-acre spread north of Minnow," the boy Wilson said. His voice had grown louder in the storytelling, his gestures more sweeping and confident. Chief watched as Wilson peddled his newfound wares: the life and times of Clayton Standard. He wondered how much of it Wilson knew to be true and how much of his story was only hillbilly claptrap, cast down through the leathery lips of some brother or uncle who claimed to have known Standard when they were mere runts coming up in the holler, who claimed to have been standing in the shadows when he burned Mandell's Seed to the ground, who claimed to have helped him dump the kerosene, to have spirited him away afterward on a borrowed nag. Chief had known so little about the dead man, and still he felt he'd known enough. Now and then, he turned his back to the story because of how unlikely it seemed.

"The Mandell homesteads were scattered across a fine stretch of timber," Wilson went on. "Nice houses they'd built off the same plans, water closets, and indoor cookstoves. Houses for families. Dogs. Barn cats running around in the yard. Each brother kept a chicken coop in his field. And the land up there? Incredible! You could turn around southward from anywhere and see clear to Minnow, clear to Wolf Hollow, even, away out on the Elkhorn River. I've been out thataway a few times, got a few customers out there myself. When there ain't no clouds at night, the moon'll light that part of the country up just as though it were lunchtime. That's the way it was on the night Clayton Standard went out avengin. Bright as day, though it was well past midnight.

"The way I heard it is that he snuck into Thomas Mandell's barn with a mind to find something he could use to slit the fat man's throat. He rummaged around a bit and come up with an old curry comb what was so rusty and dull, it wouldn'ta broken a man's skin if he was fresh outta the bath. He slipped it in his back pocket, anyway. Then he came across a set of sheep shears, the old spring-loaded kind, oiled and sharpened down to a fine split. He took them outside and tested them on the necks of some sunflowers and boy, their blades musta sparkled in the moonlight. Whack! Whack! He cut the heads offa all them sunflowers, what Thomas Mandell's daughter, Sarah, had planted in the springtime. It came out later she'd given them all their own names—Lillian, Gwendolyn, Harriet, and whatnot. But Clayton Standard killed each and ever one of em right there and left em dead in the grass.

"It's said there was a lantern still burning in the house, or else it had been lit while he was in the barn; I heard it both ways. The old boy crept up to the window and peered inside and saw Thomas Mandell's wife, Bernadette, who is a chubby woman and pleasant enough to look at, standing in the middle of the room, very still like, staring at nothing at all. As though she'd frozen in place. Of course, she wasn't looking, you understand, but *listening*.

"It hadn't occurred to Clayton that anybody other than Thomas Mandell would be inside the house. He hadn't counted on a family because in all his days working at the seed supply, he'd never once heard mention of any of the men's wives, nor of their children. In his mind, the Mandells were drunken stags who went home after work and stripped naked and drank whiskey and slept in heaps on the floor. But when he looked through the window, he realized he'd been wrong. He saw a clean, well-kempt home, a comely woman in her nightgown, a spinet piano against the wall. He could hear dogs yelping in the distance, probably from Glen's house."

"This ain't fixin to be one of them terrible love stories, is it?" one of the men barked hoarsely from the crowd. "We may not look it, but I assure you ever man in this crew is a good Christian."

"I'll tell of no violence against women, if that's what you mean," Wilson said.

"That's what I mean."

"Good, then," Wilson said. "As a matter of fact, Clayton knew he needed to roust Bernadette Mandell away from her husband, so he took the curry comb from his pocket and rapped a little number on the windowsill. Then he sunk back against the house and waited. He could see above him the woman's shadow darkening the glass. She peered for a while out into the moonlight and eventually went away. So, he rapped on the windowsill again, but this time, as he'd hoped, she didn't come back.

"It wasn't long before he heard the voice of Thomas Mandell carrying on through the nighttime. The fat man stumbled in his undergarments onto the lawn with his shotgun drawn to his shoulder. 'Who's there now?' he said, 'How do you like scaring my wife, you fuckin cretin? D'you know what time it is? Come out or I'll blow your head off!' And he heard a rustle over here, and now over there, and he looked up just in time to see the curry comb flying through the air and it struck him—pap!—square in the head. Ripped a big chunk out of his skin and left his forehead streaming blood into his face. Just then, the line of brush out back started jittering, and Mandell ripped a shot into the leaves and all fell quiet for a minute. The thumping in Mandell's ears slowly began to settle. He could hear the crickets shouting in the field and the dogs at his brother's house yowling into the darkness. He thought maybe he'd killed the sonofabitch, or wounded him besides, but when he made slowly toward the thicket, he heard a voice behind him say, *Fuck the bunch of you,* and he turned and blasted a wild shot, but there was nobody there. When the smoke from his muzzle cleared, he saw nothing but a moonlit field ahead of him. But there, glinting in the grass, lay his sheep shears. No dead man's hand attached to them, and no reason whatsoever for them to have been moved from the barn.

"In the morning, Mandell's daughter came to breakfast crying. She'd been outside and seen her sunflowers lying dead on the ground. Lopped off clean. Her father had not gotten back to sleep, and his head was pounding and thick with bandages, but Sarah had little mercy for those things and dragged him out to show him the slaughtered plants. Well, he just couldn't figure it out. He stood there with his hands on his hips and cast his gaze down to the town of Minnow, where soon enough he saw a thin trail of smoke, like the tail of a rat, situated about where the feed store had used to been."

Gary Childress, who was listening intently to Wallace Wilson's story, shook his head vigorously. "I'm curious to know whether anybody mourned your boy Mandell's aim with a shotgun."

"Actually, mister," Wilson said, "Thomas Mandell was an excellent shot. Even today, he's known in Minnow as one of the skillfulest huntsmen in the county."

"Well, then, I'm curious to see how that's possible."

Wilson offered a sly, knowing grin. "The finest marksman there is can't hit a target that weren't there to begin with."

"You sayin Standard wasn't never there?" a man shouted from the back of the crowd.

"He couldn't'a been," Wilson said. "Because that morning, when they went poking around in the embers of Mandell's Seed Supply, they found a boy's bleach-white bones about where the center of the store would have been. Wasn't nothing much left of him. Some scraps of singed hair on his skullbone, a few little flecks of meat on what used to be his arms. It's thought he musta set fire to some bags of wheat chaff that Glen Mandell was holding back for a pony he was fixin to buy for his son's twelfth birthday, thinking it was grain. Well, that dry a tinder? Clayton Standard may have caught a faceful of heat and been dead and gone before the fire got off the floorboards."

Chief listened to the story and weighed it against what he knew. The other men had been doing the same: here was a stupid little boy telling them Clayton Standard was dead and had been for some years, though they themselves had buried him just the autumn past, though they themselves had eaten his biscuits, though they themselves had watched him save men's lives whose lives didn't deserve saving.

"It doesn't make sense!" Chief cried suddenly. His voice was thin and cracked, like a schoolboy's. "How'd they know the bones belonged to Standard?"

Wilson smiled. "Hell, that was the easy part. It was Elroy Halbfinger went pickin around the embers that morning, found about ten dollars' worth of melted clay chips around the body. Same ones Weepy Bingham was using at his place. Same ones Benjamin Standard give to his boy before he skipped town."

The sentiment of the crowd began to turn on Wallace Wilson. The men guffawed and spat at their feet, dismissed him with angry flips of the hand, turned to chatter with each other, to murmur their disappointment with the bullshit tale the man was weaving. Wilson stood smiling the whole time, watching with satisfaction as they riled themselves further. It was almost as though he'd been waiting years for the chance to tell the story in its entirety.

Finally, he said, "You don't believe me, fine. Fine, I said! It don't bother me none. But what I'm telling y'all is true, and as a matter of fact, it gets truer. What would you say if I told you that was only the *first* time Clayton Standard died? What would you say if I told you he come back to life not five years later and soon enough died all over again?"

IN THE MORNING, Chief stopped by Standard's hooch to see that he'd gotten some breakfast, but the big man wasn't there. He rapped on the door of the privy, but the voice that came back—"A minute, please"—was small and vaguely feline and certainly not Standard's. He tromped across camp from one side to the other looking for his friend, barely noticing the men who stood straighter as he went by, looking at him funny, casting newfound thoughts upon him, sizing him up as the foundation of interesting rumors they'd heard from the mess-hall cooks.

"Tender," they whispered to each other. "Cookie described it as *tender*."

"Said they had a *moment* together."

"Said he raised his mitten-hand up and gave Chief a little pet, like."

The new information was less a bomb than a brushfire; it slid across camp like a bucket of spilled lamp oil. If Chief had been a less respectable man and Standard not so fearsome and important, both of their lives in camp—and perhaps their lives *altogether*, it wouldn't have been unheard-of—would effectively have been over. But Chief had been a man of intelligence and Christian morals, and Standard one of blunt beauty and untamed aggression. They were neither of them trees for chopping down. So, the conversation about their meeting in the mess hall, though persistent as a mosquito bite, never quite burst open the way such conversations sometimes do.

Chief found Standard in the one place he shouldn't have been: the field, working alongside his clan. He'd stripped his bandages off and was swinging an ax with his raw, ravaged hands, grunting with effort and pain, while a pair of exhausted cross-cutters stood behind him, marveling and whistling at his superhuman ability. Chief watched Standard from the treeline, his great body torquing and stretching like a cat's, the rapture of his long hair dancing when the ax blade struck meat, the final elastic draw of his stance before he pulled away for another swing. In no time at all, Standard had become efficient and cocky; when he struck a particularly solid blow, he sometimes turned to the men behind him and smiled. *Yeah, yeah, motherfucker,* they'd say, laughing and shaking their heads, *Yeah, yeah, yeah.*

Chief had a mind to come down from the woods and berate the big man for his selfishness, to come at him shaking an angry finger and cast him back up to camp, to banish him to a convalescence of boredom and solitude, but it just wouldn't do. For one thing, it assumed he had any real control over Clayton Standard, which he clearly did not; the man wouldn't follow a simple order to rest, even after having his hands nearly torn away. Also, to sunder the oaf would only eat away at the tenuous morale Chief had managed to cobble together since the Baltimore decree: Standard, simply put, was good for business. The greenhorns saw him and wanted to be as good as him; the veterans saw him and knew they'd *never* be as good as him but swung a happier ax for it, anyway; Standard drank the admiration of both groups and became stronger. Like Samson, his hair continued to grow. Chief decided his attempt to curtail Standard had been foolish in the first place.

He watched the men working for a few more minutes, eager to see the tree fall, eager to see if Standard's gunning was true. From where Chief stood, it looked like the hickory might catch the brambled limbs of a younger tree that rose twenty or so yards north of it; if it did, they'd have a hell of a time getting them untangled. A tree snared up with another was a dangerous thing: to get them untwined required more guesswork than was comfortable and a patience most men didn't possess. Standard chipped toward the notch of holding wood in the center of his cut, and when he reached it, he stepped away and the cross-cutters took over, setting their blade on the opposite side of the tree and drawing a line across the trunk and jamming a wedge into the gap it made. Standard delivered a couple sharp blows with the hand sledge and cried *"Tamberrrr!"* and the tree groaned and its top shimmied and it gave way with a ripping sound, the trunk tearing from the stump and dredging a rut in the soft soil and the treetop swishing through the air and landing in a straightaway just right of the hickory Chief had worried over. It fell flat on its face like a drunkard collapsed in a gutter, shaking loose a cloud of dust and mites and bark lice and feathers and birds' nesting and, when all was settled, Standard looked up into the treeline where Chief had been watching, knowing somehow he was there, and smiled.

Yeah, yeah, motherfucker, Chief thought.

HETTIE STANDARD WAS FORCED to accept that her son was dead, a fact which she grieved over terribly, and that her husband would probably be gone forever, a fact which she did not. She lived on in the cabin in the woods, went on teaching in the one-room schoolhouse, skipped a garden the first year after the fire but raised one every subsequent summer; to not grow her own food was both too expensive for her meager salary and too hard on her soul. It meant something important to be outside in the new morning sunlight, feeling her disappeared husband's heat on her neck, listening to the wind that sometimes spoke the words her son might have spoken had he still been alive. She'd felt like a coward that first year, a termite holed up in its dank wooden sheath, but to be back in the greater world proved, if to no one other than herself, that she wasn't afraid of that world, that as long as it continued to spin, she would continue to spin with it, even if all the spinning made her heartsick and drunk with wanting.

In his impulsive actions, Clayton Standard had ensured that the townsfolk of Minnow would not go suffering alongside Hettie, and she was surprised to find herself fine with such an arrangement. She wasn't the same criminal as her boy had been, but she'd raised him and so she was close. They allowed her to go on teaching mostly because there were few other folks who qualified, and the ones who did had long ago aged out of any desire to put up with twenty rapscallions six hours a day, to chop wood for the potbelly stove that squatted in the center of the schoolhouse, to confer with the hillbilly parents of children who weren't their own and who they ultimately cared little about. So, Hettie continued to walk the three miles to work and three miles home, five days a week except for summer and the ten-day Christmas recess. Along the way, she watched the seasons change, the sky turn its different colors, the storm clouds form and dissipate, the trees burst forth in the spring and burn themselves out in the autumn. She was not sad, exactly, but instead, simply lacked any dream for the future or plan for her own wellbeing— and was oddly satisfied by it.

"There are two different men who stare down the barrel of a gun," Wallace Wilson said from his perch atop Clayton Standard's casket. "The one who worries that his life is not yet finished, and the one who rejoices in having done all he could."

Incidentally, Undersheriff Halbfinger, the man Benjamin Standard rode half to death in Weepy Bingham's faro parlor, had stopped visiting Hettie Standard. Instead, he went around town dirtying her good name, claiming sometimes that she'd never told him she was married and other times that he'd never fucked her in the first place. His face stretched into a look of abused indignation when she came up, as though every time he heard about her was the first time. Everyone knew, though, that the real reason he stayed away from the Standard homestead was that neither he nor his father had managed to catch up to Hettie's good-for-nothin husband, and as far as Undersheriff Halbfinger knew, that scrappy bastard might this very minute be hiding in the hayloft of Hettie's barn, or under the floorboards of her porch, waiting for Halbfinger to come back and try to say something else. As was becoming her pattern for everything save her young boy, Hettie didn't miss *him,* much, either, though if you'd asked her in private, she might have admitted she had once enjoyed his attentions.

It was Christmastime when Clayton Standard came back. Hettie woke that morning to a new snow, a whitewashed world outside that made her smile as soon as she saw it: she loved the weather, after all, considered a good snow God's best foot forward. She opened the door into the yard and laughed to see a white, doughy crust up to her waist. Everything was nearly covered: the blackberry hedge down the footpath, the doors to the barn, the giant slab of sandstone jutting from the grass where Clayton had once played battlefield with his tin soldiers. *All is at peace,* she told herself, and closed the door and went to fix the fire.

As the day wore on, though, odd things began to happen. Though it did not feel so cold in the cabin, a frosted skin had grown down the wall between the living area and the kitchen; she touched it with her fingertips and recoiled when it seemed it might burn her. There was trouble lighting the fire, then, too: her matches kept blowing out after the strike, before she could touch them to her tinder. She must have sat on her knees in front of the old stove for an hour or more, cursing and griping, before a flame finally took. Then she set a pot of water on for coffee and went to change into her housedress, but before she'd even gotten her arms free from her nightgown, the water had struck a raging boil and was gagging and spewing onto the stovetop and onto the floor. She pulled the nightgown free and dropped it on the floor and ran naked to the stove and pulled the pot away and stood wondering at the sizzling white puddles atop the cast iron.

"You might fix some clothes for yourself," someone said. The voice startled her and seemed to come from everywhere at once: she wheeled around to the reading chair, but there was no one in it; she peered into the kitchen door but there was nobody there, either. She instinctively covered her chest with her arm and slid closer to her bed.

"Get out of my house," she said, but it sounded more like a request than an order. She picked her nightgown up with her toes and brought it to her hand and was sliding awkwardly into it when she looked out the window and saw that the fresh snow had been disrupted: there was a canyon cut into it where someone had come up the footpath hip-deep from the road and across the front field to the dooryard. She'd neither seen nor felt anyone come inside. "Go back whatever way you came in," she said.

"You don't mean that," the voice said.

"Get out of my house!" Hettie said. "I do mean it!"

"To go away again would require a mighty big effort, I'm afraid," the voice said. "Anyway, I ain't totally healed from the first time."

Hettie Standard brought her hands to her face, standing half-dressed there in the morning sunlight, and cried out, "Clayton?"

And then there he was, standing in front of that frozen wall. Fully-formed—in fact, twice as big as he'd once been; five years of death had not inhibited his growth an inch. He stood on the nappy old rug in the center of the room with his bare toes digging into its stitching. Smiling. Enormous. He stretched his big paws out to embrace his mother.

"Now you'd like to believe, wouldn't you, that a woman might think twice in a time like this," Wallace Wilson said. "Here's a man, after all, that she only barely recognizes, who can't be but fourteen years old but appears to be twenty—thirty, even—and she goes to him like he's still that nine-year-old boy, having woken feverish from a dream."

"It's previously established that she cares for strange men," someone called, and a din of hoots and laughter rippled through the crowd.

"Shut your yaps!" Gary Childress said. "We will respect women in this camp!"

"Even whores?" someone said.

"Especially whores," Childress replied.

Wilson's mouth twisted. "Anyway," he said. "Hettie touched her boy's face and lifted his shirt and ran her fingers up his arms, and his skin was covered over with evidence of fire," Wallace Wilson said. "She put her hands on his cheeks and turned him this way and that, stared right into his eyes, looked at his harelip and put her finger on it and started to cry.

"He asked her what year it was, and she told him it was the year nineteen and ought-eight. He asked her who was president and she told him she didn't know because she didn't pay attention to such things. He asked her if she'd seen his father and she said no, thank God, that snake in the grass ain't come around since before you... well. He asked her if she'd buried him kindly and she said yes, what was left of you I buried kindly, and he told her he'd like to see the grave.

"She'd interred him away up on the hillside, up the slope running along the back of the homestead, a good hour's hike in the weather, but she rustled herself into a pair of her husband's woolen britches, and they started out anyway. The day was bright, and the snow had quickly gone icy. What would have been a difficult traverse on flat land became near impossible on a grade, and when Standard saw his mother struggling for purchase, reaching for sapling trunks and cursing under her breath, he crossed over and swung her onto his back and rode her up the hillside thataway.

"They had to dig for a while to uncover the stone. Standard took a step back and looked at it. It was small and rounded at the top, like a tablet of testimony. It bore but seven words: *Here lies Clayton Standard, simple heathen child.* 'Can't say I'm proud of the epitaph,' he said. Hettie explained to him that the stonecutter she'd commissioned had not followed her instructions on the wording. She'd asked him for 'Here Lies Clayton Standard, loving son' and he'd agreed, at first. When she'd returned with her cart, this is what he'd created instead. The look in the stonecutter's face told her it was a point not worth arguing. 'I even give you a word for free,' he'd said. She hadn't been able to afford a replacement. She hoped time would eventually wear away the lettering.

"'Anyway,' Clayton Standard said, pointing at the stone. 'I guess there ain't such a huge gap between that and the truth.'"

Near the beginning of that autumn season when the boy Glick killed Clayton Standard in a fistfight, a posse of armed hillbillies crested the camp road with their mess tins jangling on their belts and their drawls leaking out the sides of their mouths. They were a dozen or more, a group meant to fight but not meant to fight for long: dusty, thin at the belly, and carrying the hunch of desperation around their necks. Chief met them on the road with Gary Childress, Chappy, and Standard, all of whom carried cocked rifles at half-shoulder.

"Stop there," Chief called.

The unfamiliar men hesitated in their formation and glanced at one another, puzzled, as though Chief's instruction had come in a foreign language. A few of them breathed heavily through bandannas, and others wore beards so long you could not make out their mouths. Then one of them cried, *"Hup!"* and they marched onward. Standard raised his rifle and aimed at the man who'd called it, as he was the one who seemed to be in charge. The cluster of them were about as far away as a child could throw a milk bottle.

"You're on private land," Chief hollered. "We're within our rights to defend it." At this, Childress and Chappy also raised their weapons.

The leader of the posse made no motion to halt, and his men came up with none of their own accord. Chief stood square in the center of the road, but though the ragtag group came ever closer, he, too, ordered no action.

"Chief?" Gary Childress said. "What if they pull?"

Chief licked the beading sweat from his lips and hoisted his Remington.

"Chief?"

"If they pull, we unload," Chief said. "We unload if they pull."

The men alongside him seemed to take a crazed sort of permission from this, and each set and sighted his rifle.

"Blue shirt left," Chappy whispered.

"Double-handles there, in the center," Childress said.

"The rest of them motherfuckers," Standard said, and the other men smiled and snorted laughter across their gunstocks.

Still, the bedraggled pack moved forward, seemingly oblivious to the threat of four rifles centered on their chests. Some of them shuffled their feet, and it was only then that Chief looked down and saw that most of those feet were bare. *Confederates,* he thought, but too late: some motion had been perceived by a man in his group, some hand on a bent man's hip, and his boys took their shots and the rapport of rifle fire rounded into the air and deafened all of them as though they'd sunk in a balloon to the bottom of the sea. When none of the posse fell, they chambered their rifles and fired again. The sound dampened by the sound of the first. The men remained upright, coming forward with their guns still holstered.

"Now, goddammit," Gary Childress said. He looked at his weapon as one would a disobedient mutt, as though he'd have liked to slap it senseless. "This motherfucker." Then he shouldered it and fired again, as did Standard, as did Chappy, each with the same result.

Chief, for his part, held his weapon by his hip. "Ain't really there," he whispered, but his boys were deaf with gunfire and couldn't hear him.

Childress and Chappy and Standard all took several steps forward. By then, they were almost within arms' length of the group. They tossed their empty rifles onto the roadside and raised their fists and made to fight.

Chief, though, held back. All sense in the situation had burned away among the rifle fire: no man was so brave as to face down a hail of bullets without pulling his own weapon or, barring that, coursing for the nearest tree; this pack of men should have been no exception. There was another reason for their inaction, and that reason, it seemed perfectly logical to Chief just then, was that they were no longer connected to the earth as they'd once known it and were therefore not reacting in any particular way to its sights and sounds, to its odors or weather, to commandments from men they could neither see nor hear. They were simply fulfilling a destiny, a destiny set for nearly fifty years by then, to traverse a world they could not recall, to try and go from one place to the other in the hopes that the other would be lit by stars, the pattern of which they might finally recognize.

With the lead man finally close enough, Standard reared back and swung a great haymaker toward his jaw and watched his meaty fist dissipate the man's humors like a cloud of breath: the man's head exploded into a thousand speckles of gray light and drifted on a breeze through the tree branches above. At the same time, Gary Childress had lined up a kick to another man's groin and watched in stop-time as his foot chopped the man's light neatly in half and he fell away into two sections, like a hand and the reflection of a hand cut catercorner by a pool of water.

"What in the goddamn hell," Gary Childress said. He looked back to Chief, who stood behind them with a drowsy look on his face, as though the whole thing had exhausted him.

The prostrate troupe passed through and around them like wind. They'd made no effort to fight, and indeed the only indication they'd given that Chief had addressed them—that little pause in their march— may well have been nothing but a collected memory, a thing they'd been doing habitually for years, a pause after a certain predetermined number of steps. A hitch in their routines that they hardly even noticed anymore.

It may have been that their lead man barked *"Hup!"* a dozen times a day, and it didn't much matter whether that *"Hup!"* led them into a firefight or a whorehouse or the coal-dark field of a country cemetery.

Chappy and Childress and Clayton Standard retrieved their weapons from the roadside and walked past Chief, who stood motionless more or less in the spot where he'd started. They shook their heads and reached to pat his shoulder and in so doing, suggested that they'd never actually believed they were seeing what they were seeing, that he was the one with the vision, that he was the one who'd get to tell the story in whichever way he saw fit.

Standard lived with his mother for the next several years, doing the labor a husband should have done but that Hettie had proven herself more than capable of. They worked at their hard lives together. They shored up the leaning barn, constructed paddocks for the ducks and piglets Hettie'd always intended to raise, planted corn and pole beans and a dozen new varieties of tomatoes. Clayton got up on the roof with a bucket of pitch and patched up the leaky spots. He mixed a pail of mortar and fixed the chimney. They even painted the window frames.

Hettie tried not to think too much about what was happening. She couldn't. To accept it as anything other than a miracle would have condemned her to insanity. Here was her delightful, beautiful boy— again!—and not much changed except his being so big that he was almost two of himself crammed together; except that he had the long, greasy hair of a young man and a deep hollow in his voice, as though when he spoke, he did so from the inside of a pignut hickory. Not much changed at all, except his knowing how to pitch a roof, the burning vendetta he carried against his father for leaving Hettie broke and alone, the sense of invincibility he assumed due to having died and come back to life. No matter. Hettie still saw in him her little boy, the one she'd read to in the lamplight until the wee hours. Maybe it's an ability unique to mothers to have missed a son for years and, at the reunion, to learn all the things he now knows, all the things he's seen and can now speak on, the scars he's earned, the hobble he's acquired in his gait, the women he's loved and broken, the skeptical bend of his eyebrow when a plate of something good is offered up, and still say, *My son, thank God, you're the same, you're the same, you haven't changed a bit.*

They took three meals a day together, simple affairs always: hambean soup, duck eggs and fried potatoes, chunks of raw summer squash with vinegar.

On Saturdays, they loaded the cart, and Hettie drove it into Minnow to hawk their garden vegetables at Parlak's General Store. Mr. Parlak always bought up almost everything because the vegetables were beautiful and so was Hettie Standard. As soon as word went around that her husband had split, each of the bachelors in town lined up to take their crack at getting Hettie into bed with them, despite being skeptical of her lineage and mildly unnerved by ghost stories they'd heard from Thomas Mandell. Some of their attempts were more easily parried than others, but Mr. Parlak's effort had been among the most persistent. He was a thin, handsome, fragile-looking fellow with a thick head of Turkish hair graying above the ears, always nattily dressed with a waistcoat and pleated slacks and a pocket watch on a chain. His wife, a country girl named Wendy Strait, had died in childbirth and left Mr. Parlak with a baby boy and a unique last name in territory that could be hostile to the unfamiliar. Hettie allowed him to cast his line, let him flash his brilliant smile when the bell above his door tinkled and she walked in with an apron-load of tomatoes, put up with his simpleminded commentary about how lovely the sun-dark triangle of skin at her cleavage was because her very being rested on his continuing purchase of those tomatoes.

One Saturday, she and Mr. Parlak, finished with their business, stood at his counter trading flirtations. She clutched a small wad of paper money and allowed the hair that had fallen loose from its bun to stray as it wished; whenever she laughed, a little too theatrically, at something Mr. Parlak said, the hair slid farther down her back. She made no move to fix it. She knew Mr. Parlak was very fond of her hair, and so she never failed to wash it on Friday evenings, knowing he'd have something to say about it the following day as he reached into his till and fished out another dollar for her to take home. "For the trouble," he sometimes said, or, other times, "For rights of exclusivity." They both knew that he meant two things by *exclusivity:* the one she was willing to give and the other a simple *maybe* she could dangle over his head while she went on stretching him like a handful of taffy. He had just handed her this extra dollar on that particular Saturday when the bell above his door tinkled and Elroy Halbfinger walked in, hiking his britches and coughing up a load of phlegm, which he spat onto the floor.

"Sheriff," Mr. Parlak said. "Good morning to you."

"Undersheriff," Halbfinger corrected. He did not look at Hettie or at Mr. Parlak but cast his eyes back and forth across the shelves as though he'd come in for something but couldn't remember what.

Hettie took an instinctive step backward. She'd not seen Halbfinger close-up in several years. His face was mottled and doughy, as though he'd taken a load of buckshot from a good distance, and the scars had healed poorly across his cheeks. She remembered him as a strong and shapely man, but now his gut bulged haphazardly over his belt. His feet, swollen with last night's liquor and straining against the seams of his shoes, seemed to lag a beat behind the rest of his body. Hettie found herself grossly mesmerized. She wondered if Halbfinger had always looked so poorly. She wondered if she'd simply imagined him differently when she'd allowed him to push inside of her behind the barn.

"Lookin for a deck of cards," Halbfinger said, still refusing to acknowledge Hettie's presence. It occurred to her that maybe she could just leave, tuck Mr. Parlak's money into her apron, and slide around Halbfinger and out the door without his ever knowing.

"I don't carry gambling utensils," Mr. Parlak said.

"Why's that?"

Mr. Parlak frowned. "My profit's slim enough without God's judgment getting involved."

Halbfinger made a clucking sound with his tongue. "How about just a band of ponies?"

"I'm afraid I don't carry smoking utensils, either," Mr. Parlak said. He shrugged apologetically. "Same reason."

"No smokes and no cards, huh?" Halbfinger said, hitching his pants again. Hettie thought how desperately he needed a set of suspenders. "I suppose a pint's too much to ask, in that case."

"Far too much, I'm afraid," Mr. Parlak said.

Halbfinger hung his head and laughed. "Last night's not gotten outta my system yet," he said. "Have we had this conversation before, friend?"

Mr. Parlak forced a smile. "Many times over, Sheriff. Or something like it, anyway. I assure you, though, I don't mind."

"Undersheriff," Halbfinger said.

"Undersheriff, yes," Mr. Parlak said. "One day I intend to get that correct."

Halbfinger burped loudly. "Don't bother," he said. "One day I *will* be sheriff, and you won't look like a horse's ass no more."

Mr. Parlak folded his fingers together and rested them at the center of his waistcoat. "Is there anything else I can help you find, Undersheriff Halbfinger?"

Halbfinger snapped his eyes up from the floorboards and trained them on Hettie for the first time. His mouth was wet with saliva, as though he'd been drooling or was about to vomit. His cheeks were flushed with blood. "You fuckin this n——?" he said.

"Elroy," she said.

"The law demands to know, Hettie Standard."

Hettie sighed. "You're not worth talking to just now, Elroy. Why don't you go and sleep it off?" She shoved her hands into the pockets of her apron, so he wouldn't see them shaking.

"Why don't you come with me?" Halbfinger said. He ran his tongue along the inside of his lip, and she could see it there like an animal trying to burst out.

"Sheriff," Mr. Parlak said, "Not to be rude, but—"

It only took Halbfinger three disorderly strides to reach the counter. He shot his arm out and snapped Mr. Parlak up by the throat and lifted him off the ground. The well-polished toes of Mr. Parlak's shoes scraped across the grit on the floor, and he hacked spittle and snot across Halbfinger's sleeve. Hettie screamed and slapped at Halbfinger with her hands.

"Where's your fuckin boat?" Halbfinger snarled, cocking his head sideways to look into Mr. Parlak's face, which had already gone pale.

"No boat," Mr. Parlak said.

"No boat?"

Mr. Parlak's eyes fluttered.

"You'll need a boat."

"Why?" Mr. Parlak croaked. His head had begun to loll like an infant's.

Because you're going home, that's why."

Parlak's eyes rolled back and he seemed about to pass out. He mouthed a *fuh-fuh* sound over and again, his teeth scraping against his bottom lip. He might have been trying to say "Fine." He might have been trying to say "Fuck you."

Elroy, drop him!" Hettie said.

"Not til he tells me he'll get a boat," Halbfinger said. Hettie watched the tendons in his arm ripple as he tightened his grip. Mr. Parlak was losing his life; that much was clear.

I'll take you again," Hettie said. "Let him down, and I'll take you again. Right now. However as you please."

Halbfinger opened his hand, and the choking Mr. Parlak fell onto his backside and leaned against the shelves, clutching at his throat and sucking air through his brilliant white teeth.

"*Ya ibn el sharmouta*," the handsome shopkeep grunted. He hung his head between his legs and retched a thick band of saliva onto the floor.

"You just hang onto that cockamamie Latin," Halbfinger said. "We ain't through here."

"Yes, you are," Hettie said. She grabbed the bulbous finger of one of his hands and pulled him out the front door. "Come on, you fat pig. We're going home."

"Poor bastard don't know what he's got comin," Gary Childress said. "Wait til he finds out what kinda venom our boy Clayton's got in his veins." He slapped Standard's wet coffin, and soon enough, the others joined in, slapping and pounding on the pine box as though it were a war drum. They smiled and hollered. Chief looked to the old fishermen beside him and saw them laughing. Their fish hung from bits of snipped line, mouths gaping wide as if they, too, were celebrating.

Wallace Wilson stuck his hands in his pockets and waited. His story was coming to its end.

THAT EVENING—fire dying, ghost story told and retold, men dissipated into the nighttime—Chappy and Chief and Clayton Standard sat with long sticks in their hands, poking at the coals. Gary Childress had long since gotten drunk and retired to his hooch for the fitful sleep of a maniac.

"'Twas a hell of a thing, that," Chappy said. The flames danced in his glossy eyes like nymphs, and the smoke from his cigarette trailed into the whiskers of his mustache.

"Make you believe any different than you done this morning?" Standard said.

"Not at all. In fact, my faith runs stronger now than ever before."

Chief felt a frustration well inside himself. "Now, just how is that, exactly?" he said.

"Everything that was ever done," Chappy said, "the Good Lord intended to be done. By decree or by freedom of will, there ain't nothin happening on Earth that God didn't see comin."

"And so?" Chief said.

Chappy relaxed in his chair and blew a great plume of smoke into the black sky. "And so, that a specter, or for that matter, an entire *pack* of specters, should walk the Earth—it's the business of God and God alone to understand. It's no more ours to explain than the vastness of the sea, or the love we hold for our women. What we know is all we need to know."

"That sounds real nice," Chief said. "But I'm afraid it don't explain the newfound depth of your conviction."

Chappy closed his eyes, and for a minute, Chief thought he'd fallen asleep. "I understand most everything that happens in this camp," Chappy said finally, keeping his eyes closed. "Hell, I believe I understand most everything that happens in the whole world." He took a drag from his cigarette and spit out a fleck of tobacco. "I once saw a swinging hickory limb remove the top half of a man's body from the bottom half in one clean swipe. Fellow was minding his own business, which I suppose was his first mistake, thinking about the sweet thigh-flesh of some schoolgirl back home, or about how he'd be spending his money come the weekend. Either way, he didn't hear the warning, and the branch hit him in the belly and tore his entire innards in twain."

"Gareth Shepherd," Chief said. "I knew that boy."

"Shepherd was indeed his name," Chappy said. "I watched fifteen men run over to that boy and try to put him back together. They picked up his guts and tried to stuff them back into his belly, but he was split from top to bottom, and the guts just poured back out again, right into the dirt, with nothin to hold them in place. The boy's eyes just a'blinking. His mouth still popping open like a caught fish." Chappy pitched his cigarette butt into the embers. "Took several minutes for him to die, as I recall."

Chief sat thinking about Gareth Shepherd for a while. He'd been in camp that day but had not himself seen the boy's accident. It had been his second week in charge of the operation, he'd been busy and disoriented, and when a group of men brought the bloody chunks of the body to him, he'd rushed behind his hooch and puked. It wasn't the first time he'd seen a man who'd lost his life, but it was the first time he'd felt responsible for it.

"Finish your point, Chappy," Chief said. He glanced at Standard, who hadn't moved in nearly an hour. The big man held his stick limply at the fire's edge, watching its ember grow closer and closer to his hands.

"My point is," Chappy said, "that while what happened to Gareth Shepherd was tragic and gruesome, it was entirely within my capability to understand. A man made a mistake in a dangerous place and paid for it with his life. It's a callous truth that death is so predictable a part of life." He laid a paper on his knee and dipped a pinch of tobacco into its fold. "Some folks turn to God to help them understand death. As though every time a man loses his life, it's something new and incomprehensible. Me, I need no such solace. There are them who pray for *more*—more money, more food, more health, while other folks pray for protection for themselves or their families. I'm here to tell you that all of them prayers get answered. It's just that most of what gets prayed for is common, simple, unremarkable. There is nothing so exceptional about a bushel of corn appearing on a hungry family's doorstep."

"But a troupe of rebel ghosts?" Chief said.

Chappy laughed. "Now, there's the sort of thing that'll remind you," he said. "God's got the stuff."

CLAYTON WATCHED FROM THE WINDOW as Hettie steered her cart up the hill, an uncomfortable-looking Elroy Halbfinger in the back with his big legs crossed like a child, and his eyes cast stupidly to the sky. His mother looked up to the cabin and cocked her head to the side, and Clayton moved away.

She pulled the cart against the side of the barn and unhitched it and walked the mules into their stalls. Halbfinger sat in the back, watching the day pass with the hungry look of a street urchin: the midday sun had chapped his lips, and crusts of salt from his sweaty forehead had gathered in the folds of his eyelids. Now and then, he lapped his dry tongue around in a circle like a dog whetting itself for supper.

Hettie came out from the barn and clapped the straw dust from her hands. "Come on, then," she said.

The undersheriff wrenched himself from his seat. He stepped gingerly from the cart and bent to crack his spine. "A fine day," he said, his voice suddenly sober and jovial. He hitched his pants and took a minute to take in his surroundings, glancing up to the house, to the chicken coop, and to the hayloft door, which was closed and cinched tight with a cotter pin.

"I ain't seen him in years," Hettie said.

Halbfinger's hand went instinctively to his nose, which remained gently off-kilter from his run-in with Benjamin Standard. "Hell," he said, "it ain't nothing to me. If he shows up, I'll blast him in his face."

"Okay, then," Hettie said. She turned and headed toward the back of the barn, kicking her shoes into the grass and lifting her thin cotton dress over her shoulders. It had been a long time since she'd bothered with undergarments.

The season was old enough by then that the weeds were stiff and thick. Honeybees buzzed at her feet, scattering from flower to flower and away to the trees; grasshoppers bounced up from the switchgrass and clicked against her skin. The sun was hot on her back, and she could feel that soupy brand of summer sweat breaking in her folds. This was to be an unenjoyable tryst. She thought of Mr. Parlak and briefly doubted he was worth it.

Behind her, Halbfinger's boots plodded like dumb beasts through the grass. She hoped to God he wouldn't see fit to take them off. His grunting—lord, how she remembered it now. The snorts of a boar in rut! The extra weight that hung on him like a satchel of rancid meat! She closed her eyes and sighed and bent double with her hands against the rough wood of the barn.

"No, no," Halbfinger said. "We'll be doin this one different."

She stood and turned. "Well. I said what I said."

Halbfinger smiled and wrenched the button free on his trousers. His pistol was tucked haphazardly into the waistband; he was too lazy to wear a belt, and therefore wore no holster. He pulled the gun and laid it on the woodpile Hettie and Clayton had stacked the autumn before.

"What's first?" he said.

"It's your day," she said, and spread her arms away from herself. Her skin was slick. Hitchhiker seeds dotted the hair on her arms and legs. "I gave you my word."

"I done as you told me to do, didn't I?" he said.

"You did, and I'm grateful."

He took a step closer. "You're in love with that loose-talkin Arab, ain't you?"

"Love is a catching disease," she said. "I done recovered once. I don't intend to contract it again."

Halbfinger pulled his trousers down to his ankles and took her by the wrist and laid her hand on his foul pecker. "Maybe I can change your mind," he said.

"I doubt it."

He moved her hand carefully back and forth. "You got a heart of stone, you know that?"

"It was men like you made it that way," she said.

Halbfinger barked out a laugh. "Alright, well. Best get on them knees."

She looked at him a moment longer than she wanted to. Over his shoulder, far back in the woods: movement. Her son, shifting from tree to tree with a shotgun tight against his chest, gaining ground as quietly as he could.

"That ain't no way to do it slow," she said. "You'll finish in two shakes." All Clayton Standard needed was time. All she needed to do was stall. She believed deeply in the revenge her son would bring.

"That's of my concern," Halbfinger said. "Get on them knees. I ain't asking again." She saw Clayton nod his head quickly and pull the hammer of his gun.

"Well, if that's what you like," she said. She drew a deep breath and fell to her knees quickly. At the same moment, Clayton fired and the hair on the back of Elroy Halbfinger's head lifted, and he stumbled forward. Hettie batted him away and stood and looked up. A circle of barnwood blown away, just above where the undersheriff's head had been. Standard had missed.

Halbfinger stumbled with his trousers still around his ankles and snatched his pistol from the woodpile and cocked it and fired a single shot into the trees. Then he wheeled around on Hettie. He reached up and fingered the back of his head. He'd been struck by stray pieces of shot, and his hand came back bloody.

"What was that?" he said. His eyes were red and bulging. "Woman. I said—"

"Fuck you," Hettie said.

So Elroy Halbfinger, still a little drunk from last night, raised his pistol and centered it on her chest and shot her, just where her stone heart would have been.

WALLACE WILSON HAD BROKEN the collective heart of the camp.

"Wait!" a man called from the rear. "You're telling me Hettie's *dead?*"

"Dead as a hung pig," Wilson said. "Story Halbfinger made up is that he never left with Hettie at all, and it weren't til later he went up there to apologize for his behavior in Parlak's store. According to him, that's when he found the bodies. Murder-suicide, he called it."

"Goddamn!" the man called. "I was gonna strike off to find her when we was through here."

The others chuckled but only quietly because the man wasn't really joking. Most of them had thought a similar thing.

"That shot he fired hit Standard?" Chappy called out.

"That it did," Wilson said. "Hit him square between the eyes. Felled him like a sack of corn, right into the leaves. He was likely dead—dead *again,* that is—before his ass even touched the ground."

There was a din of emotion from the crowd. They mumbled *No* and *It can't be,* they told the kid Wilson to *Fuck off.* They were used to stories that ended the way they wanted them to end: with the vengeance of the oppressed, the poor bastard striking gold, the hooker who could blow a man to smithereens. Their very favorite stories ended in orgasms powerful enough to douse fires, a boss-man's castration (literal, preferably, figurative if nothing else), the angry father watching from his rich man's porch as the hillbilly captured his daughter's heart and swept her into the mountains. They wanted their heroes to have *persevered.* It was how they wished to see themselves, after all: as conquerors, explorers, traffickers in bravery and honor. They viewed themselves as a modern army: in the future, all the important wars would be fought against Mother Nature, and these men dug their trenches deep in the Appalachians, a beachhead against the sea from the east and the violent dust clouds of the Western prairie.

It's the curse of every working man to believe his profession more important than it is or will ever be.

"Say," someone called out, "this Halbfinger fellow still alive?"

Wallace Wilson smiled as though he'd expected the question. "That story I just told y'all is fifteen years old by now. Halbfinger's been the sheriff of Lancaster County for more'n ten of em," he said. "Lives right down in Minnow. Ain't but a half-day's ride from here."

"Maybe we can go meet him someday," Gary Childress said.

COME TO THINK OF IT, on the day before the boy Glick killed Clayton Standard in the waters of Cranberry Creek, there had been some sort of row in the mess. Tables overturned, kits spilled, men in their longjohns taking blind cuts at patches of air where faces sometimes were. Gary Childress had been there, and Chappy, and Standard, and the boy Glick, who sat with a handful of other greenhorns. The old versus the new. Experience versus energy. One of the kids had said something about Chief that didn't sit well with the veterans, and experience had stood to teach energy a lesson.

The fight spilled out into the daylight, the men grappling and grunting, their hands and faces soaked with gravy and chopped spinach. They took huge, lumbering cuts at each other—mostly missing, blinded as they were by the sun and the bits of food in their eyes. Standard fought alongside the vets, though he wasn't much more than a greenhorn himself; his soul was old, after all, his body ragged with scars. None of the youngsters begged him onto their side. Instead, they did what they could to avoid him. Every now and then, though, he caught one by the shirt collar and slung him around a bit and flicked his rag-doll body back into the melee like a rat onto a dance floor. A demented smile on Standard's face: it must have seemed to him then that all of life was in good fun.

After a while, the brawl dissipated, as fights will. Combatants exhaust themselves, the thirst for water grows intense, the desire to gloat about a supposed victory overwhelms the desire to earn the victory in the first place. Some of the battered contestants shook hands with their adversaries, some spat globs of blood into the dirt and laughed. Old men clapped young men on the shoulders and followed them inside to clean up their mess.

Chief had come up on the fight as it happened, the dogs at his heels with their old tongues lagging behind. It wasn't something in which he saw the need to intervene. A fisticuff like this might lose a man a tooth, sit a man out for a day with a twisted ankle, but invariably, it would also serve to reaffirm the camp pecking order, and that was always of good use to a smart foreman. Besides, the jacks were mostly being gentlemen; nobody, as far as he could see, had pulled a knife or gone along throwing punches with a rusty dowel pin in his fist. The fight seemed surprisingly even, actually. Though the camp elders were outnumbered two-to-one, the six or seven of them still somehow managed to hold their own. To interrupt their nonsense would have become a political act: in stopping a fight, the vets knew they were winning (or, at least, weren't *losing*), Chief would be halting the resurrection of their pride, the absence of which could have very real consequences later on.

But then, as the other men stood and dusted their caps and traded lewd barbs with one another and wandered into the mess, Chief saw something strange. Standard and the boy Glick had hung back. Just for a second, barely long enough to blink, but Standard had said something, Chief was sure of it, and Glick had responded. Then they'd patted their hats on the knees of their britches and gone in to help the others.

As unceremoniously as he'd jumped on, Wallace Wilson jumped back down from Clayton Standard's coffin. His story was over, but his audience was not sated. They followed him up the hill to his cart, pegging him with questions about the Standard homestead and where it was, where they could find the tombstone, where he thought Benjamin had run off to, whether Glen and Thomas Mandell had ever gotten theirs. Wilson shrugged his shoulders as he went about the work of loading Chief's belongings into his cart. "If I'd known the answer to that," he said, "I'da told it in my story."

The cool blue light of early evening had come on by the time Wilson tarped and cinched the cart. Some of the men had patted Chief on the shoulder and wandered away to drink, others had gone back to the creek to fish in the twilight. Chappy stayed behind as a sort of vigil to Chief's leaving, as did Gary Childress, though his was likely a sense of obligation more than one of mourning. To see a comrade off with reverence was simply good management, and Childress needed the practice.

A stone's throw away, the rough-hewn end of Clayton Standard's coffin rested in the new mud of the creekbank. The men had dragged it ashore and left it, agreeing to re-bury it on higher ground in the morning. But now, its body lifted and swayed in the swells; before daybreak, it would dislodge itself and float away again, and Standard would be free to haunt some other place, some place downriver where the boys who found him would not yet know his story. Chief carried his bedroll to the cart and set it behind the seat for the dogs to lie on and looked down at the coffin. Its wood slimy and split. Its rusty, repurposed hinges. When they buried Standard, they'd cinched it shut with twists of steel wire, a defense tipped toward superstition more than anything else, though Chief could appreciate the unintentional wisdom in it: without those few strips of metal, it would have been Clayton Standard himself, and not his coffin, that had gone drifting aimlessly in the current.

Chief hung on the view longer than seemed necessary. He couldn't get his muscles to do what his brain needed them to do.

"Would you mind excusing me for a minute?" he said to Wilson.

Wilson, sitting in his saddle atop a gray-speckled mule, smiled around his cigarillo. "You take what time you need," he said.

So, Chief took ginger steps down the slope to where the coffin rested and laid his hands on top of it. There could be no true knowing, really—not in this life, anyway—what Clayton Standard had meant to him, but he suspected in that moment that whatever his debt to the younger man was, it was one he would never find the means to repay. Standard had defended his station in life with the only type of energy he possessed: brute strength. He had grown enormous on it, and confident, and the backward men he'd come to know in camp had respected him for it. They'd eyeballed his physique over their cans of cold beans and their games of cards, hooting and whistling in jealousy and wonder and fear. Until the day he died—the day he died *again,* that is—Standard had used his strength to the best of his ability and never pretended he had any other benefit to offer. The men had been right to respect him. The blind man uses his blindness to sharpen his sense of smell. That's what Clayton Standard had done.

But the men were not representative of the world, and the world did not respect the same things anymore. It had become a place of calibrated mechanics, of unthinking devices that could chop trees without the distraction of lives to bother their work: machines, after all, could not have memories, would never have drinking problems, could not possibly look forward to seeing the same little curly-blond girl again over the weekend, could not be rendered senseless by the way she'd looked with her dress bunched around her waist. A machine would sit in the dust with its little mechanical face dead-still, and its pistons would fire until the job it had been positioned to do was done. Then it would be repositioned. It would never laugh at any jokes, even if a man or two stayed behind to tell them.

Chief closed his eyes and did something he hadn't thought to do when they'd buried Standard the first time: he prayed. He prayed that the young man had found peace; he prayed that his hardship was over; he prayed that this was the final time he'd have to die. Three times, it seemed to him, were plenty. A man should not have to defend honor to the death over and again. There must be a point at which a just God would draw the line and say, *Never mind you now, there ain't nobody listening.*

On the other hand, maybe that point *had* come, maybe several times, and Clayton Standard had just been too stupid to understand it.

What little light was left fell into the gaps between the wood staves of Standard's coffin, and Chief peered into it without really thinking. There wasn't much to see there. A tangled mass of bramble and detritus. A shifting mountain of mud. He could see no bones, no hair, no fingernails, but it was no great revelation; in a way, he wouldn't have been surprised to open the coffin and find that Clayton Standard was no longer inside at all, though he prayed this wasn't true.

"Happy enough to go?" Wallace Wilson said, watching Chief make his slow way back up the hill.

"Happy enough," Chief said. He whistled sharply, and the dogs leapt onto the cart and settled down on their old haunches. "Well," he said, looking down at Chappy and Gary Childress, men who were not his friends but had usually been close enough. "Kiss my ass goodbye."

"An honor to be in your employ, Chief Haymarket," Gary Childress said. He tried to smile, but his teeth were small, and it made him look demented.

"I wish you the best of luck, Childress," Chief said. He looked out onto the forest as though he might consume it all in one breath. "I fear you'll need all you can get."

Childress laughed and kicked the ground. "Hell, if I'm here another two years, it'll be damn near a miracle."

Chief supposed he was grateful that the old hand at least knew his fate.

"Well," he said again. "Mr. Wilson, if you please."

"*Hyup!*" Wilson called, and snapped the leathers across the mules' backs. They stumbled forward like a steam train on a cold start.

As Wilson turned the cart onto the road that led over the hill, a great blast shattered the evening air and made the mules skitter forward. Chief turned and saw a wild-haired pack of his men holding the smoking barrels of their rifles skyward, their position one of informal salute. He watched them standing there until the cart crested the hill and he couldn't see them anymore.

WHEN THEY PULLED STANDARD'S BODY out of the creek, Chief had come to see him at the waterline. A nervous energy buzzed in his bones, and he pulled his stinking hat off to hold it over his heart. They rested Standard in the marshgrass and wiped their hands on their pants, backing instinctively away: to pat a living man's shoulder was not the same as gripping a dead man's wrists. Somewhere in the interim between living and dying, an essential substance had departed, the extant warmth that made it okay to feel a person's flesh. Some of them made faces and turned, snorting, from the body.

The boy Glick, wrapped against the tree and with the pale skin of his cheek slowly peeling away, bellowed like a calf, claiming a miracle, claiming God's intervention. He who had once been weak had been given an undue measure of strength. Well. Maybe the boy was right. Maybe it was divine.

Chappy had come down and said a prayer. He stood over Standard's body and read loudly from his Bible.

The men chipped at the earth with their tools. It was bad luck to let a corpse lie around too long.

Chief stood quietly working his hat brim in his fingertips. Clayton Standard had been a work of art, he thought, a loyal dog borne from the Appalachian mud whose sense of justice was unmatched, if also unrefined, and whose work ethic was rivaled only by his dangerous confidence. Chief couldn't help but think of the way things were going: soon enough, his horses would be replaced by gasoline engines and his men by stout, sputtering machines, and those men would go home to make more babies who would soon enough also wander into this dying frontier, a place where there had once been jobs for a man who could swing an ax or shoe a horse, but which would now require him to go underground and eat his meals in the pitch-blackness and set off explosions so that he might haul away the hellfire that rained down on his head.

Soon enough, Chief thought, they'd make machines that could do that kind of work too.

His final words to Clayton Standard had been spoken the day before he died, several hours after the dust-up at the mess.

"Glick boy wants to fight," Standard had said. They were walking the crest trail from camp to a flat bottom where work would soon begin. "Fair enough. A greenhorn's got to show out for his boys."

"He doesn't know what he's talking about," Chief said.

"Probably thinks I challenged his honor."

"You didn't."

"No. In fact, it was him challenged *your* honor."

Chief stopped. "I don't give a damn, Clayton. Boy doesn't know me from Adam."

"A man who'll challenge your honor without knowing you is an especially dangerous kind of man."

"That may be so."

The bottomland was quiet around them, the air heavy; there was rain coming.

"You don't think it's worth the lesson?" Standard said.

"No," Chief said. "I don't."

"Can I ask a question? In your reckoning, what *is* worth the lesson?"

Chief looked up at a seventy-foot hickory that would likely be among the first to fall the next day. "In my reckoning, Clayton," he said, pressing into the tree's skin with his fingertips, "men weren't really designed to learn lessons."

WILSON WAS AN ERRATIC DRIVER. The closer they came to dead nightfall, the harsher he whipped the mules. Chief found himself gripping the rough corner of his plank seat, now and then looking back at the dogs, who'd grown anxious and unsure of where to rest themselves. The cart's wheels chucked and whinnied, and he only hoped they'd hold fast long enough to get him where he needed to go.

"Some story you told back there," he offered, hoping to catch Wilson's attention. The driver seemed to have fallen into a sort of trance as he steered.

"Ever word of it true," Wilson sad.

"How is it you come to be so familiar with the details?" Chief said. The commotion of the cart coursing through the forest forced him almost to shout.

"It's a tricky piece through here," Wilson said. He drew the reins tight to his chest and the mules surged forward. An angry raging from their noses, and their hooves slapping harder on the mudpack. The cart caromed out of its turns, and Chief had to lean crosswise to keep from falling off.

"I ain't in that much of a hurry," he called, but Wilson was not listening.

They were as far away from camp as Chief had been in years. He could tell because of the smell of the loam, the tang of the earth that was kicked up by the cart's wheels, the unfamiliar shapes of leaves, and the surprising knots of branches that blocked the moon from shining full. They sped past underbrush whose density he could not recognize. The glowing yellow eyes of predators off in the deep woods, their hungered purrs shuddering, disturbing the moonlight that surrounded their bodies. He could smell water close-by, could almost taste the spray kicked up by invisible rapids, could run his dirty fingers through his long hair and lick off the dew they brought back.

Despite the forging darkness, or perhaps because of it, Wilson whipped his mules harder until they coursed like thoroughbreds. The glass lantern he'd lit and hung from its hook swung parallel to the ground, blown as it was by the torrent of wind the mules threw as they ran. The dogs whimpered and groaned and spread their legs at odd angles, trying to gain some purchase on the ragged carpet Chief had thrown across the cart.

Chief, though, felt an uncommon calm in his bones. He considered that Wilson's recklessness was of the practiced sort, and he developed a confidence in the man that was completely undeserved but complete nonetheless. He simply clutched the rope handles affixed to the buckboards and let the boy do what he knew to do.

Without warning, Wilson craned his neck and called, "I forgot to thank you for the business. Things have slowed since the railway came to Minnow."

"You didn't mention you was coming from Minnow," Chief said. His voice trailed into the woods like a breath of smoke.

"Born and raised," Wilson said. "Don't know how long I'll get to stay, though. I suppose you know as well as I do that the world's changin."

"That it is," Chief said. "That it is."

Wilson smiled over his shoulder, and in the wavering lamplight, Chief could see the crooked little dimple that formed there, though the scar that caused it was covered over by his mustache.

HERE IS THE THING THAT NOBODY KNEW—not Chappy, nor Childress, nor the Pennsylvania Dutch boy Glick, nor even Chief himself, for certain: on a Saturday night when the men were down in Summersville and the snow was falling silently on their camp, building its slow fortress, and the dogs were sleeping happily in the floor of Chief's hooch, Chief and Clayton Standard had pressed their mouths together. It had been brief and surprising to them both. If there were a witness, he might have called it a kiss, but Chief could not be sure that's what it was. He could not be sure it bore the hallmarks of a kiss—that it had been tender enough, that there had been any kind of sexuality attached to it at all. What it felt like, mostly, was a resuscitation. An exchange of life from one body to the other. One of them had been saved by the gesture, or perhaps both of them had been; twenty-seven years later, Chief would die without ever knowing for sure.

IT WAS A STONE THAT OVERTURNED THE CART. Standard had steered them too sharply around a bend and a wheel had caught on the rock and the whole apparatus tipped violently sideways. The dogs had tumbled off into the bramble, and the mules had rolled and whinnied, the weight of the cart driven through the pole shaft, snapping their backs and buckling their legs beneath them. Once things had settled, the animals lay braying and twitching in the ditch, having kicked up a cloud of dust and crickets that blew off and sparkled in the moonlight. Somewhere in the underbrush, the dogs whimpered.

Chief shook himself loose from a tangle of ruins and stood. He felt mostly well but patted himself up one side and down the other to be sure he'd not sprung any kind of leak. The wheel of the cart spun uselessly in the air. One of his boots had fallen off, and he'd no idea where it was.

He found Wilson wrapped like a sheet around the trunk of a young sycamore. His impact with the wood had been violent: his eyes had popped nearly out of their sockets and, through the grimacing mouth, Chief could see that some of his teeth were missing. Thick blue veins bulged on his forehead like earthworms in a dough.

Chief stood for a minute looking at the body. The dogs, tender but walking, came warily to his ankles, as though he himself had been the one who'd done them harm. He bent to scratch them behind their ears, to try to regain some of their trust. He looked up at the sycamore Wilson had chosen to die upon: a lovely specimen, if too young for harvesting. It would make someone's children a fine rocking horse someday. They would never suspect the death that had gone into it, and it was better that way.

Acknowledgments

Josh Gesner, Sharon MacNeil, and Amber Jackson all read early versions of this story. They gave me plenty of suggestions to make it stronger and all the encouragement I needed to keep writing. I can't thank them enough.

I'm so lucky to have found the team at April Gloaming, who treat each project with immense respect and bring a beautiful energy to making good books. Thanks to believers like them, indie publishing is alive and thriving. May they all live long and drink good wine.

And, as always, I'm grateful to my partner, Elizabeth: incredible teacher, awkward hugger, and the mother against which all other mothers should be judged. Thank you for building a room out of time and space where I can hide every day to write these weird books. Love, love, love.

Author Bio

Josh Patrick Sheridan is the author of the novel *Old Fires*, available from April Gloaming Publishing. A native of West Virginia, he now lives with his family in upstate New York, where he teaches writing at the State University of New York at Albany.